THREE
GO SEARCHING

THREE
GO SEARCHING

By
PATRICIA M. ST. JOHN

Illustrations by
ROBERT G. DOARES

MOODY PRESS
CHICAGO

Copyright ©, 1966, by
THE MOODY BIBLE INSTITUTE
OF CHICAGO

ISBN: 0-8024-8748-3

Paperback Edition, 1977

Printed in the United States of America

CONTENTS

CHAPTER 1

"As Lights in the World"

IT WAS BEDTIME. Murray and David sat curled on the big bed in their pajamas while Dad read to them as he did every evening. But tonight was different from any other night because it was the last time. Tomorrow Murray was going to boarding school by plane, hurtling away into the blue all by himself to be met by his grandmother at the other end. David was not quite sure how his brother felt about it.

Of course Murray had been very grand and boastful, and when the school uniform arrived David had felt green with envy. But now Murray sat very straight and still, cross-legged on the bed, his thin young face flushed pink, his fair hair standing up in spikes because he had just had a bath. His hands were clasped tightly together and his eyes fixed rather sadly on his father. Dad too seemed to be very much aware that tomorrow Murray would be leaving them.

"I'll give you four minutes to see if you can learn that verse by heart," said Dad, handing the Bible to Murray. "I want you to remember it all the time you are at school." And because David disliked being forgotten, he butted his head under Murray's elbow like a little goat and tried to learn it too. The words were rather long and difficult but

Dad had just been explaining what they meant. It was
Philippians 2:15: "That ye may be blameless and harm-
less, the sons of God, without rebuke, in the midst of a
crooked and perverse nation among whom ye shine as
lights in the world."

There was dead silence for four minutes by the clock.
Murray's lips moved silently while David puffed and wriggled. He wished they could hurry up because they were
going to have a last-night feast, and Mother and Joan were
ready; he could hear them whispering in the next room.
But at last Murray handed the book back and repeated
the verse perfectly without a mistake because he was ten.
David joined in where he could because he was only eight.
He would be nine in a couple of months.

A few minutes later they were ready to join Mother and

Joan in the living room. They all sat down on a rug around a little table about nine inches high. It was a delicious feast: salted peanuts, cookies, orange soda, and french fried potatoes—in fact all the things Murray liked best; and because he would not be with them for Christmas, they lit a candle in the middle and turned out the lights, and for a quarter of an hour they were all safe and together in the charmed circle of candlelight. The children were as merry as could be, and none of them guessed that Mother and Dad, who seemed merry too, were thinking in their hearts: *This is the last time that we shall ever be quite like this. When we see Murray again he will have learned so much about the world beyond the candlelight; perhaps he will feel too old to enjoy little feasts in his pajamas.*

It had come to an end at last because Joan's curly head was nodding and the candle had burned low. They washed their sticky fingers, brushed their teeth, and jumped into bed. Mother knelt long beside Murray, talking in a low whisper while David, who had been hastily tucked in and kissed, lay wondering whether he would be glad or sad when his time came the following year.

In the morning everything was a rush and bustle as they had to get to the airport by half-past eight, and it was a long way out of town. Dad, who was a doctor, had to say good-bye while they were still having breakfast, for he had to go over to the hospital; so it was just David, Joan, and Murray, all huddled together in the front seat because no one wanted to be so far away as the back seat, as Mother drove out to the plane. Ragbag the puppy wanted to come too, but he did not understand airport regulations and was better left at home.

It was very hot on the concrete area where they waited. The plane was there, all ready, a beautiful silver creature with blue propellers. On any other day they would all have been thrilled, but today the minutes seemed to be running away; they just could not be stopped.

The awful part, thought David, was that Murray seemed to have shrunk. In his ordinary clothes, his khaki shorts and T-shirt, he had seemed a large, strong boy with fine, strong muscles. But in his new gray trousers and black and red sports coat, bought slightly too large to allow for growth, and the school cap that came down over his eyes, he looked like a perfect shrimp. David could hardly believe his smallness, dressed up in those generous-sized new clothes. He thought, *Whatever will I look like next year?*

The voice from the loudspeaker began telling the passengers to board the plane. Murray, rather pale, flung his arms around his mother's neck and clung to her just for a moment. Then he kissed the top of Joan's head, squeezed David's hand, and was gone, running across the asphalt after the other passengers, clutching his attaché case and passport, his new raincoat trailing on the ground. Neither hand was free to mop up the tears that were streaming down his face. He got smaller and smaller, until he disappeared altogether inside the silver body of the plane. They saw the stewardess stoop down and speak kindly to him, and a moment later he reappeared at a window and waved. He had wanted a window seat very badly, and he had found a handkerchief, so no doubt he felt better. A few minutes later the propellers began to turn and the great machine moved majestically down the runway, turned, stopped, came back with a rush and a roar, and rose to the blue. David knew that Murray wasn't crying now. He would be watching those wings and propellers and had probably, just for the moment, forgotten all about everybody.

But down on the hot asphalt it was lonely and flat. Mother's eyes were brimming with tears, and David had a strange ache in his chest. Only Joan, who was fat and impervious to sorrow, was jumping up and down on the weighing machine, enjoying herself. They went back to the car and drove home almost silently through the hot countryside from which all traces of green had vanished— nothing but cracked clods blistering under the burning blue; and David was saying to himself, *I don't even care if it's a jet or a comet! I don't want to go away alone like that and not see Mother for a year—Oh! why do we have to live in another country? Why can't we all go home to England and see Murray again at Christmas?*

He suddenly could not imagine why they had not all thought of this beautiful, simple plan before. It seemed so easy. He thought about it all the way home, sticking his head out of the window, liking the breath of the hot wind on his brown cheeks. He did not mind that Mother did not talk, for he knew her thoughts were far up in the blue sky somewhere above the sea. Joan did not mind either. She had climbed into the back and was jogging up and down singing a song that had no tune or rhythm—just happy words.

They swung through the big double gates of the hospital compound and went across to the house. It was cool and shady indoors, and they all sat down in the kitchen and had a snack to comfort themselves. And when they were all settled with milk and cookies, David suddenly leaned his elbows on the table and said, "Mother, I don't want to go away from you to another country. Couldn't Dad be a doctor in England now, and then we could come to you every holiday, and you could come and see us on Saturdays. It was so nice in England, don't you remember, Mother? Then we could all be together always. You ask him, Mother."

David's mother did not answer for quite a long time. Joan lolled against her shoulder, and Mother rested her chin on the brown curls.

"We can't do that, David," she said at last. "You see, we were sent here like soldiers are sent by their king. A missionary is a person who is sent."

"Sent for what?" asked David.

"To tell people who don't know, that God loves them and that Jesus died to save them, and to show them what a Christian should be like. Jesus died for all these people but none of them know it yet. We've got to tell them and show them the way."

"Couldn't you do that in England?" pleaded David. "Oh, Mother, do ask God to send you to England. I don't want to go away so far."

"But there are lots of churches and Christians in England," said his mother, "and anyone who really wants to know can buy a Bible and read it. If everyone stayed in England it would be like having lots and lots of candles all burning together in one corner of a big dark house and all the rest of the house pitch-dark. The darker the place the more it needs the light, and although we hate your leaving us, Dad and I are glad that we were sent to such a very dark place. There are hundreds of towns and villages out here where the people can't read and have never heard of Jesus as Saviour at all. That is why Dad and the nurses work so hard. If there weren't a hospital, the people wouldn't come, and if they didn't come they would never hear."

"Lots of little candles!" repeated David brightly. "That's like Murray's text last night. Do you know it, Mother—about a crooked and 'averse' nation, and shining like lights in the world? Dad taught it to me and Murray last night. Mother, can children be missionaries?"

"Certainly," she answered. "The most important part of a missionary's work is to show what a Christian should be like: as different as light from darkness. When you play with the other children, remember that. Show them that a Christian is kind when others are cruel and selfish, and truthful when others tell lies, and self-controlled when others lose their temper. They will soon wonder why, and perhaps you might even get a chance to tell them. But always show them first. A light is made to be seen."

There was a rustle in the passageway, and a little, brown, thin face with dark eyes .nd black curly hair peeped around the door. It was Waffi, their next-door neighbor, and David looked at him with a new sort of interest. Up to now they had played with the neighbor children but always together. Murray had been the leader and David had followed, just one of the gang. Now he realized that he must stand on his own feet and find his own playmates because although he was very fond of Joan, she was too small to count. There would never again be anyone like Murray, but perhaps he and Waffi could have some fun together. Waffi was about his own age, as far as anyone could remember, and quick-witted and adventurous. The language he sometimes used was most interesting too, al-

though fortunately David could not understand quite all
he said.

Black eyes met blue eyes in a long cautious stare. David
turned to his mother.

"Can I go to play with Waffi?" he asked. "And can we
play on the beach?"

Mother glanced down at the shingly beach surrounding
the little bay at the bottom of the turfy slope. "Yes," she
answered, "down there, where I can see you, and I'll ring
the dinner bell over the fence a quarter of an hour before
dinner time. Ragbag can go with you."

It was fun slithering down the path that led to the bay.
David in his sandals was no more nimble than Waffi bare-
foot. Ragbag barked with relief. He had felt that something had been very wrong with the family, going off like
that and leaving him tied to the doorknob! They had all
smelled as though they were in low spirits and, anyhow,
where was Murray? But scampering down to the beach
like this seemed cheerful and ordinary again. Ragbag
leaped in the air and snapped at a butterfly.

The beach below the house was a lovely place. The
water was warm and shallow, and lazy waves lapped on little hot rocks. It was a wild deserted strip of coast and
hardly anyone came here except fishermen, for the proper
beach, with miles of smooth sand and hundreds of people
and bathing huts, was around the headland. But little
boys, who did not mind the steepness of the cliff, liked
this beach better, for there were rocks sticking far out into
the water and exciting little creeks and caves which no one
but boys knew about. David's father sometimes came down
with them on his day off, and he and Murray and David
would swim out in goggles and hunt for winkles on the

boulders underwater. Winkles are delicious boiled in salt water, extracted with a pin, sprinkled with vinegar, and eaten with bread and butter.

"Let's go out to the end of that rock," said Waffi, "and climb right around to the other side. The tide is out and we can almost stand in that funny little creek."

David flung away his sandals and left Ragbag to guard them, for Ragbag disliked rock-climbing. When a wave jumped at him there was nothing to do but retreat because if he jumped back he fell into the water, and that sort of fight was no fun at all. But David and Waffi loved it, and, clinging with their fingers and toes, they clambered along the ledges where the sea anemones clung and the water came gurgling up in the crevices. It was a still day, and there was not a soul to be seen from headland to headland.

David loved this rock. There was a great cleft at the end of it into which he could swim at high tide and paddle at low tide. The jaggedness of the creekbed made the waves rather rough and he had never seen fishermen out on the end of it. He thought it was his very own creek because he had discovered it. He had shown it, as a favor, to Murray and Waffi. Sometimes he missed his footing clambering along the slippery sides and fell into the sea, but that did not matter in the least, for David could swim like a fish.

He had reached the place where the rock divided, and peered downward into the creek. Then he gave a sharp little exclamation of indignant surprise.

An iron ring had been hammered into the rock, and a small boat lay chained between the boulders.

CHAPTER 2

The Ship That Sailed
in the Dark

Pirates!" said David.

"Smugglers!" said Waffi, who knew more about it.

Both boys fell silent and remained hanging over the fissure peering down into the little boat. David longed for Murray. Murray would have known no more about it than he did, but Murray would have known exactly what to pretend and how to extract the last drop of mystery and thrill and imagined danger out of the situation. But Waffi did not have much imagination, and David felt rather frightened. He glanced up the cliff and hoped his mother was watching him from the window.

"I think it's nearly dinner time," said David. "I think we ought to go home. Perhaps it is just a fishing boat."

Waffi shook his cropped head. "Smuggling!" he said emphatically. "They are doing it all the time. My father drives a truck and the police are stopping them all along the main roads. They caught a man the other day with a load of hay, and they tore it to pieces. Inside were guns going to the frontier. We'll watch that little ship and, remember, don't say anything to anyone."

They came back along the crest of the rock on all fours, like crabs, and flung themselves on the sand to rest. The hot September sun beat down on them, but the breeze from the sea was pleasant, and there were all sorts of things to watch. To the right of them the harbor wall stuck out beyond the headland and a great American battleship lay anchored in the bay. Far beyond that they could clearly see the lighthouse against the blue. They burrowed their legs in the sand and tried to make flat pebbles bounce on the surface of the sea until the bell rang at the top of the cliff.

"It won't take you fifteen minutes," said Waffi.

"Never mind, I want to go now," said David, fastening his sandals. He did not know why, but he felt strangely glad to be climbing up the cliff again. He would have gone straight home over the back fence, but Waffi wanted to take the long way around by the road and to visit the store. He had a few cents in his pocket and wanted to buy some bubble gum.

When they had nearly reached the road, they saw a little girl lying under a fence in the shade, fast asleep, with two big baskets of grapes beside her.

Waffi stood very still and looked at the grapes; David looked at the little girl. She was not sleeping peacefully at all. She was tossing and muttering, and as she turned over he noticed that she was a hunchback and her legs were too small for her body. Ragbag sniffed at her dubiously and lowered his ears sadly.

Waffi looked around furtively, tiptoed up to the grapes, and stuffed a handful into his mouth. Then he broke off a bunch and tried to stuff it into David's mouth.

"We mustn't; it's stealing!" said David, backing away;

but Waffi had no patience with that sort of thing. "You're a silly frightened baby," he whispered scornfully. "You were afraid of that boat; now you're afraid of getting caught. If you are afraid of everything, go and play with your little sister, and I'll go and play with the big boys. They are not afraid of anything. Karem took a melon the other day, a great big ripe one, right from under a store window."

David felt all in a muddle. He longed to be a brave, tough hero like Murray had been, but he was sure Murray had never stolen anything. It would be dreadful if the boys would not play with him, and he was left alone. Perhaps there were different ways of being brave; but until he could think it out perhaps he had better take the grapes. He held out his hand.

"All right," he said gruffly, feeling very unhappy, "give me some. I'm not afraid any more than you are."

"That little girl won't wake up," said Waffi. "She's sick. Look, she's tossing and talking in her sleep! Here, have some more. They are nice, ripe, juicy ones."

They squatted on the ground, tossing the juicy purple fruit into their mouths. Having once stolen, David thought he might as well go on. The grapes were very nice and there were plenty of them. But he was wondering who could have left such a sick child alone under a fence. The flies were crawling on her eyes and lips and she looked very uncomfortable indeed. But he was not left long in doubt. Ragbag suddenly leaped up and started barking, and a black-bearded man from the country appeared around the corner, followed by his wife who carried a baby on her back.

Waffi saw him in time. His life had been spent darting and dodging and he did it now. He shot into the middle of the main road, almost between the man's legs, and after that only a greyhound could have kept up with those scudding brown feet. But David had his back to the couple and had hardly realized what was happening before a horny hand had gripped him by the neck.

"I'll get the police on you," said the man, screwing David's head around and aiming a well-directed kick at the little black dog who was barking so furiously. Then, seeing the frightened blue eyes, he realized that this was no child of his own race and became more cautious.

"Who are you?" he asked gruffly.

"The doctor's son," answered David trembling all over. "I am very sorry—I only took a few."

A gleam of interest came into the swarthy face. Still holding David firmly, he prodded the little girl with his foot. "Get up!" he shouted.

The child, awake by now, only moaned and tried to lift her head; but it fell back against the turf. The woman looked sorry and crouched down beside her.

"It's no good, my husband," she said. "The child cannot walk, and we cannot carry her and the grapes and the baby and the empty baskets. If you want to get back to the village tonight you must leave her behind. They have shut the door at the hospital and they will say we are too late; but if that is the doctor's son, send him to fetch his father to speak to us. When they see her they will take her in. They are compassionate people."

"I'll find my father," said David eagerly, only too glad for a chance of turning the man's attention away from himself. "Come with me, and I'll show the way."

"Good," said the man, who was impatient to get home. "You, woman, stay here and guard the fruit. And you, boy, take me to your father and I'll say nothing about the fruit; but if you fail me or deceive me, I'll call the police."

He picked up the girl and followed David along the main road. Waffi was nowhere to be seen. The big hospital gates were closed, but David knew a way around. By hook or by crook, he must get in to his father.

"Wait there," he said to the man, pointing to a low stone ledge by the gate. Then he hurried through the garden and slipped into his father's clinic through the back door. There was still a little crowd of people waiting to be seen, and Dad was going to be very late for dinner as it was.

"Dad," said David, pushing through the group of patients and reaching the table where his father sat, "I've got a sick little girl for you."

"Not the first," said his father, pausing a moment to look at him. David's shirt was wet and muddy, and his hair stood up in a cowlick, very fair above his brown forehead. His eyes were wide and very blue, and his snub nose covered with freckles. He was not really allowed in, but perhaps it was something important.

"Where did you find her?" asked Dad. "And what's the matter with her?"

"She's sick," said David, "much worse than all these people; and her father kicked her."

"Very well," said Dad, "bring her in and I'll look at her." David darted away, and a few minutes later all three returned, the man determined to be rid of his burden as soon as possible.

"She's nothing to do with me," he said, holding her out. "Her mother and father both died of typhoid fever last year, and it is a pity she did not die too. What place is there in the world for a hunchback child without parents? No one wanted her, but my wife feeds her, and she helps in return. Today she started out to market with us, carrying a basket of grapes, but she became sick on the way. I could not carry the grapes and pomegranates so I left her to rest under the bamboo. When I came back, after I bought a sack of grain, I found her like this. And how can we carry her and the grapes and the baby, as well as the grain and the baskets, back to the village? Besides, she is not ours, and we don't want a sick child in our home."

He held out the little creature as though he would like to drop her. The doctor took her from him very gently and laid her on a couch. She lay very still now and did not seem to hear or care that no one wanted her. She might have been any age. Her twisted body was very small, but her face looked old and careworn. David felt a lump come into his throat as he looked at her, and he turned and ran out of the room. She was quite safe now. Dad and the nurses would look after her.

Mother was looking for him as he ran down the path. "You're late, David," she said. "It's more than a quarter of an hour since I rang the bell."

"I couldn't help it, Mother," he panted. "I had an adventure. I found a poor little girl with a lump on her back and she's very sick. Nobody wants her, and the man kicked her, so I took her to Dad. Don't you think, Mother, when she's better she could come and live with us? Nobody else wants her."

His mother smiled. "I'll go and see this little girl," she said. "I expect someone takes care of her. Wash your hands for dinner now. Is Dad nearly ready?"

"No," said David, "there are still lots of people. We found a little tiny secret boat, chained between two rocks. Do you think it might be smugglers?"

"I expect it's a fishing boat," said Mother, tying on Joan's bib. "Come and sit down, David; we'd better not wait. Yes, Joan, I'm listening, but eat your soup first and then tell me the rest."

Joan was trying to tell a long story about a cat who had had kittens behind the garbage cans, a rather unhealthy spot where children were not meant to go, but which had now become the center of attraction for all of them.

David let her prattle on as he ate his dinner in silence. He felt very unhappy and lonely. Murray had gone, and they would not see him again for a whole year, which was almost as long as forever. There was that little girl lying so still, and nobody wanted her. Worst of all, he had stolen those grapes, and he could never tell anybody. Perhaps he would even have to go on stealing, because Waffi liked stealing and would call him a coward if he didn't, and would tell all the other boys. He suddenly pushed away his plate. "I'm not hungry," he said. "I think I feel sick." But as soon as he had said it, his father came in.

"Well," said his father, "how did Murray get off? He'll be over France now."

They went on talking about Murray, and Joan went on talking about the cat behind the garbage can, not minding much whether anyone was listening or not. David got up and leaned against his mother's shoulder, and no one thought it strange that he should be sad. They were all feeling sad because Murray had gone.

"By the way," said his mother at last, "David was telling me about a little sick girl. What is the matter with her?"

"I'm not sure yet," answered David's father. "She's been taken up to the wards and I'll see her again after dinner. She's very ill and thin and neglected. I don't know if we can do much for her, and the sad part is that even if she does get better she doesn't seem to belong to anyone. She's just a little servant girl."

Waffi, rather sensibly, did not turn up after dinner nor the next day until the evening, and David felt half relieved and half worried. He didn't like Waffi much: Waffi had not only stolen but he had also run away and left David alone with the man. Yet life was pretty dull without him or Murray. None of Murray's other friends had been to pick him up, and Joan only wanted to play with dolls or visit the cat with the kittens. He had built himself a wigwam with bamboo sticks in the garden but it wasn't much fun alone; and, on the whole, when Waffi's sly little face peeped around the gate about sunset, David was not sorry and was ready to let bygones be bygones.

"I can't stay," said Waffi, who had not been invited to stay. "My father sent me to the store and he'll be at me if I am not back quickly. But this morning I went down to the beach early and the little boat was gone. It didn't go in the daytime either 'cause I watched from the top of the cliff all the afternoon and evening. It went away in the dark, David, without any lights."

"How do you know?" asked David. "Weren't you asleep?"

"Oh, I kept waking up and looking out of the window," said Waffi most untruthfully. "I told my father, and he said, 'Watch that little boat.' So David, we must go every day, and tomorrow ask your mother if she'll take us up the mountain to cut fishing rods. If we go down and pretend to fish just around the corner, it will not look as though we are watching."

David was impressed. This was real adventure and his heart warmed to Waffi.

"All right," he said, "I'll ask her. Come after breakfast tomorrow."

"I'll come," said Waffi, and disappeared through the gate in a hurry. David sat in the entrance of his wigwam with Ragbag's head resting on his feet and looked out over the sea. Away to his left, where the coast jutted out into the ocean, the sky was aflame. Then the rosy clouds paled and it began to grow dark. One bright star burned out over the headland. Just one! The darker the sky grew, the brighter it shone. Soon there would be others. *If only Waffi was not such a bad boy!* thought David. He did want to be good, but it was so hard being different—shining like sons of God, like lights in the world. He got up and went in. The dew was falling and the long white flowers of the tobacco tree, which only smell in the dark, were already scenting the dusk.

"Come along, David," said Mother. "It's bedtime. Get undressed, and don't forget to wash your knees. They're black."

"All right," said David. "Then will you read me Murray's verse about 'shining like sons of God' and the 'inverse' nation? I can't remember it."

"Yes, we'll find it when you are ready for bed," said Mother. "Joan's nearly finished. Get into bed quickly, and I'll come."

"What does it mean, Mother?" David asked when she had read the verse to him, sitting on his bed.

"It means," she said, "that you may be good and do

right, being a son of God and so like Jesus that no one can
find fault with you, not even when you are with bad people—still shining like lights in a dark place."

"But what's a son of God?" asked David.

"You are our son because you were born to us and you
share our life," answered his mother. "A son of God is
someone who has received Jesus, God's Son, into his heart
and so shares the very life of God. There's a verse that
says it: 'But as many as received him,' meaning Jesus, 'to
them gave he power to become the sons of God.' It's a
wonderful thing to be a son of God, His very own child,
sharing that beautiful shining life of Jesus which is like
a candle shining in an empty lantern. It is the only way
to be a light in the world."

Mother waited quietly for a minute or two. David was
butting his head against her shoulder, as he always did
when he wanted to tell her something that was troubling
him. But he wasn't ready yet, and he was very sleepy, so
she said his prayers with him, kissed him, and tucked him
in, and then she turned to look at the empty bed beside
him. Murray would already have gone to bed in a strange
new dormitory. He would be wearing his new, blue-
striped pajamas that he had chosen himself.

"Mother," said a drowsy voice, "can you take us up the
mountain in the morning to get fishing rods? There was
a little boat, and it sailed away in the dark without any
lights—and, Mother, tomorrow I'd like to be a son of
God—"

And David was asleep.

CHAPTER 3

"These Are Mine"

I T WAS A PERFECT MORNING for going up the mountain, and Waffi was peeping and peering through the hedge long before they had finished breakfast. There was no need to peep and peer because everyone knew he was there but he was a child who loved mystery, and to have walked openly in at the gate would have spoiled the whole feeling of the day.

They could not start at once because David's mother had to wait to tell Marian about the dinner and the shopping. Marian was a gentle woman with a sad, patient face, who had come to work for them every morning for twelve years. She had carried Murray, David, and Joan on her back when they were babies, fastening them on with a towel, and had loved them just as she would have loved her own children who had died. She would cheerfully have given her life for the family, but she had just never thought that punctuality mattered much, so it was after ten when they finally drove through the gates—Mother, David, Waffi, Joan and her doll, Ragbag, and a basket containing lemonade and cookies for a snack.

David loved the mountain road. It twisted around the slopes so that he could look back and see it winding below. On the right rose the steep hillside, but below the land stretched away toward the valley, with high mountains against the blue horizon. Mother had to drive very carefully around the bends because goats with their little black and brown kids kept skipping across the road with equally irresponsible little shepherd boys behind them. There was not much traffic though, and David's family had a special place halfway up where they went for picnics.

In spring it was like a garden, but now in the dry season there were very few flowers. There were clumps of gray, rustling eucalyptus trees that made pleasant shade, and slopes of sticky shrubs smelling sweet in the hot air. There were also sturdy little bushes and saplings growing on the slopes, and when they had all had their snack and had chased away the goat who wanted to share it with them, Mother settled down with some mending. Joan started to build a house for her doll. David, Waffi, and Ragbag climbed the hill in search of fishing rods.

It was very quiet on the hillside. They scrambled from tree to tree, looking for a suitable wand. Suddenly they heard the sound of singing—the queer chanting of the people of the land that rises and falls on three or four notes in an unbroken, monotonous rhythm. A little boy with a cropped head clad in a dirty sacklike garment sat on a rock with the goats cropping the plants all around him. He sat staring at Waffi and David with wide, unblinking eyes. He usually had nothing to look at all day long except the flock and the hillside. Seeing two boys was quite a pleasant change.

David and Waffi saw plenty of boys every day, so they watched the goats and held on to Ragbag who wanted to chase them. Two little kids were having a fight, butting each other with their stubby horns. One was much stronger

than the other, and the smaller one suddenly backed away and skipped into the middle of the road. At that moment a big truck loaded with rocks came hurtling around the corner much too fast.

The small goatherd was on his feet in a moment. He dived into the road after the kid, seized it around its middle, and almost somersaulted to the bank. There was a scream of brakes as the truck swerved over to the other side and the rocks lurched perilously. The driver shouted angrily at the child, and then the truck bolted away in a cloud of dust and gasoline fumes.

The boy lay quite still in the ditch for a few moments, clutching the struggling kid. He had scraped his knees badly but was otherwise unhurt. Then he suddenly got up, tossed the little animal up the slope, cursed the truck driver in a loud, solemn voice, and crossed the road as though nothing had happened. He gave a clear, short call, and about a dozen goats came ambling up and followed him back across the road. He sprang up the bank and they leaped behind him.

"It's enough! I'm going to take them far away from this place," he remarked to the children who stood watching, "right away on the hilltop where trucks don't come." He set off, scrambling over the rocks, and the flock crushed against each other in their efforts to keep near him.

"But you've left half of them behind," called David. "Look, there's a little one just going to stray into the road."

The boy glanced back. "That one is not mine," he said. "I only look after my own. These twelve are mine. It is enough. Those belong to another shepherd. Let them follow him." In another moment they had all disappeared into the mimosa trees, and the pattering of their little hooves on the baked earth died away.

David and Waffi found their rods and went back by way of a slippery sandbank which was great fun and left large dirty patches on the seats of their trousers. Mother and Joan had come up the road to look for them because it was almost time for dinner, and the boys came slithering down the last bit and landed with a bump and a shout at their feet.

*   *   *

The rods were a great success although it was difficult to find worms. It would be until the first rains fell. There was just a week till school started again, and the beach had become a wonderful mysterious place. A day or two after the little boat had disappeared David and Waffi ran down early in the morning, and it was back. They swam around to the end of the rock, and there it was, bobbing up and down in the creek as though it had never been away.

"It's come back in the night," said Waffi. "It wasn't there at sunset yesterday. Now we must keep watching. We'll hide down behind those boulders with our fishing rods, and one day—we'll see!"

"What shall we see?" asked David breathlessly, clinging to the rock and paddling with his legs. But Waffi only shook his head mysteriously. *Perhaps,* thought David, *he knows frightening secrets; or perhaps he knows nothing at all.* There was no telling with Waffi.

But they saw nothing. All that week they fished patiently just out of sight and once they caught a fat sardine which they fried and divided for supper. But the little boat came and went in the dark, and they never even caught sight of it on the bright horizon at sunrise or sunset, although each evening they hung over the back fence and watched till it was too dark to watch any more.

The boat filled David's thoughts. The little hunchback girl was getting better slowly, so he had stopped worrying about her, and Mother had promised that he could go see her later on. He had half forgotten about the grapes, except sometimes after dark; but he had promised himself not to listen to Waffi anymore and to be good, so he felt he need not worry about that either. After all, all he had to do if Waffi wanted him to be naughty was to say no, and that ought to be easy enough. So what happened a day or two later was rather a surprise.

They were clambering over the rocks at the far end of the beach when Waffi suddenly said, "You know that deep pool just around the bend? I've dived into it. You couldn't do that."

"I could!" flashed David. "I'm better at diving than you. My father took me out onto the raft and I dived off the second diving board, and next time I'm going off the top."

"You didn't," said Waffi.

"I did," said David.

"All right then," said Waffi, "dive into that pool from this rock and I'll believe you."

"I can't," said David. "Mother said I was only to swim on that side of the creek, where she can see me from the window."

Waffi gave a nasty laugh. "I knew you couldn't," he said scornfully. "You don't dare. I don't believe you dare at all. If you could, you'd do it. Your mother can't see you, and you'd be dry in five minutes."

He began to whistle in a most superior and aggravating

manner. David's cheeks flushed with anger. He could easily dive into the pool, and he could not stand Waffi thinking him a coward. And yet—he'd told his mother he would not. Oh, whatever should he do?

"I knew you were lying," said Waffi coolly.

"I'm not!" shouted David. "You just watch!" The next moment he had flung off his shirt and plunged headlong into the pool which was not nearly as deep as he had thought. Fortunately his arms broke the shock, but his head struck sharply on a stone, and he rose to the surface with his hands grazed badly and a big, blue bump on his forehead. He felt shaken and stunned and, scrambling out on the rocks, he began to cry.

"It's all your fault!" he shouted angrily. "I'm going back to my mother. She'll be cross with me, but I shall tell her it's all your fault."

"Tell her you slipped and fell," said Waffi calmly. "Then she won't be cross with either of us." But David was already making for home as fast as he could scramble and did not answer.

He could not climb the slope fast because he felt queer and sick and just could not stop crying, so it was difficult to get his breath. His head felt light and his legs felt heavy, and it was a very sorry, wet little figure that staggered into the house about ten minutes later, much too upset to explain what had happened.

His mother, seeing the big, purple bruise on his head, helped him into bed without asking many questions. It was already early evening and after she had put iodine on his hands and witch hazel on his forehead, she left him quieted and comforted and went to cook the supper.

His head ached, but he did not feel sick anymore and he had stopped crying. He lay there in the twilight thinking, but he could find no answer to all the questions that crowded into his mind. Why, when every day he made up his mind to be good and had even asked to be made good in his prayers, did he always do what Waffi told him? Why couldn't he say no? Why couldn't he be a light in the world, different, truthful, and obedient? He did not know. He would have to ask his mother.

He did not feel hungry, so he just lay there thinking and waiting until Mother had put Joan to bed and finished cleaning up. She came and sat down beside him. David wriggled close to her and told her everything—all about the grapes and the diving and how hard it was to say no to Waffi.

There was a little silence when he'd finished. Then his mother said sadly, "Then you just must not play with

Waffi anymore. I thought you'd help him and teach him to be good, but if he's making you to act like himself, then you must just never go anywhere alone with him. You'll have to stay here and play in front of the house where I can see and hear you all the time."

"But Mother," cried David, "it wouldn't be any fun just playing here. I'm not going to do it again. I'll say no next time; I promise I will."

"But you said that last time," answered his mother. "You can't keep yourself from doing wrong, David. There's only one way that you could ever be safe. Do you remember what we talked about the other night?"

"Yes—about sons of God."

"Yes—Perhaps you've never really asked to be made a son of God yet. Of course, in one way, God looks after you all the time and keeps you from hurtful, dangerous things around you. But sin is something inside you. Only when the Lord Jesus forgives you and casts it out and fills your heart with His loving Holy Spirit can you ever really learn to say no. You are not strong enough to shut the door against temptation; but He is."

David lay very still, listening. The warm wind blowing through the open window smelled of the sea, and the full moon was rising over the headland. The whole world seemed quiet for this special moment.

"Do you remember when we first came to this house?" asked his mother. "Some very dirty, untidy people had lived here and they would not move out till Dad made them. Then we cleaned and scrubbed and whitewashed and moved in, and the house belonged to us. But supposing one day we had left you alone in the house and they'd tried to come back and mess up everything again, could you have stopped them alone?"

"I might," said David, "with Ragbag."

"Oh no, you couldn't," said his mother. "They had a bigger dog. But if when they had tried to push in, Dad had come to the door and told them that the house belonged to him, they'd soon have run off. And it's the same with sin. You can't turn sin out, and you can't hold the door against temptation; but Jesus can. You must tell Him your heart is like a dirty house full of wrong thoughts, and you must ask Him to come in and cast them out and wash it white and be master of the house. Then you would be a son of God, and the light of the goodness of Jesus living in you would shine out to the world, and we should all see it. I shouldn't be afraid of your playing with Waffi if I knew you were a son of God, being kept by the Lord Jesus."

"Could I be now?" asked David.

"Yes," answered his mother. "Jesus has promised to come to you and forgive you and make your heart His home as soon as you ask Him; and when you receive Him, you become a son of God. You can ask Him now, David. You can become God's own child forever, now, tonight."

David slipped out of bed and knelt down as Mother knelt beside him. He told the Lord all about the grapes and the diving and how he could not be good by himself, and he asked to be forgiven. Then he asked the Lord Jesus into his heart to fill it with goodness and love and the strength to say no. When he finished he climbed back into bed and knew he had never felt so happy before in his life—not even when he had beaten Murray at chess for the first time or had dived off the second diving board with

Dad or had caught that sardine. This was a new sort of happiness that he had known nothing about till now.

"I'm a son of God now," he whispered to Mother.

"Yes, David, you're safe now and will be able to be good." She kissed him and left quietly.

David lay there thinking, and suddenly he remembered the shepherd boy risking his life to rescue that kid from the speeding truck. What had the boy said? "I look after my own. . . . These are mine." And the goats had flocked to his little bare feet and followed him up into the mimosas, jostling and butting each other in their efforts to get near him, not caring much where they went, nor afraid of anything as long as he was leading them.

Suddenly, David found himself longing for tomorrow, longing to meet Waffi, not afraid of doing wrong any more. He was a son of God now, forgiven, kept, strong with the strength of the Lord Jesus who was living in his heart and who could say no to all temptation. The "crooked and perverse nation" no doubt meant people like Waffi and the little girl and the man who kicked her, and he, David, must shine in front of them like a light in the world, like the silver moon that had swung clear of the headland and now shone out over the quiet sea, laying a silver track across the water.

CHAPTER 4

The First Clue

Would you like to come and visit Lela, the little hunchback girl, after school today?" said Dad as David rushed hungrily in to dinner, whirling his satchel by its straps, with Ragbag barking at his heels. "She's really getting over her illness now and she'd like a visitor. No one ever comes to see her."

"Oh, yes!" said David. "I've only two more pictures to stick in the scrapbook I'm making for her. I'll do that after dinner and I'll go at four when I come home from school."

His mother was singing as she mashed the potatoes, and David knew why she was especially happy: there had been a letter from Murray. He was third in his class and had high hopes of getting into the second squad on the football team. He had referred to the Headmaster as Old Eagle Eye and was evidently quite at ease and happy. They all read the letter again at dinner and David shivered with delight. Only another year, and he too would be scoring goals and calling the dean Old Eagle Eye. Then he remembered that England was a long way off and he became thoughtful. He looked around at Mother, Dad, and Joan, and out of the window at the mimosa tree and the little bay where he played with Waffi. He pulled Ragbag's ears fondly. What would it all feel like and look like without him? He could not imagine!

He hurried home after school, picked up the scrapbook he had made, and ran over to find Dad who was seeing patients on his rounds. When David found him, Dad took him to the little girl and he sat down rather shyly next to her bed.

She was propped up with pillows and looked quite different than the dirty, crying child David had seen before. She was dressed in a clean, white nightgown and her hair had been washed and plaited in tidy, dark braids. She looked happy.

"I've made you a book," said David. "I'll show you the pictures." Then he remembered she had been ill. "I hope you're better," he added politely.

"Well, yes," said Lela, rather cautiously, "but I'm not well enough to go home yet. You are the boy that brought me to the doctor, aren't you?"

"Yes," answered David.

"Well then, tell your father I'm not well enough to go home yet. Tell him my back still hurts, and ask him to let me stay here a long, long time. Oh! I wish he'd let me stay here forever!"

David stared at her. "Do you like it in the hospital?" he asked in astonishment. "I always thought people wanted to get out of the hospital as soon as they could. Do you like being sick?"

"I like being here," said Lela firmly. "I like the nice food, and the nurses are kind to me, and the bed is warm. Most of all, I like the songs we sing at night and the stories we hear about that man called Jesus. Oh! I love that man called Jesus! I want to stay here till I know all about

Him. If only He was alive now, I'd go to Him. He'd make me better."

David hesitated. He did not quite know how to explain, but he felt that the little girl had missed something. "He is alive," he said after a little pause. "You can't see Him like you could then, but you can still come to Him. I know, because I came to Him the other day."

He spoke shyly, and was hardly prepared for the way that Lela took the news. She caught hold of his sleeve, her eyes blazing with an almost unbelieving joy.

"He's alive now?" she whispered. "I didn't understand. Tell me where He is. Where did you go to Him, and what is He like? Oh! Could I go too, or do you think He'd come to me?"

"It's not like that," said David, feeling rather out of his depth. "You don't have to go anywhere. He's near, beside us all the time. I just knelt down and prayed to Him. When you do that, He can hear."

"But I can't kneel down," said Lela anxiously. "I have to stay in bed."

"It doesn't matter," answered David. "If you can't kneel down you can just lie in bed and talk to Him. If you loved Him it wouldn't matter so much about not belonging to anyone and not having a father and mother. You'd belong to Him. He'd love you and keep you safe. Ask the nurse to tell you. Look in the scrapbook; there's a picture about His coming alive after He'd died. He went to His friends who were all so frightened and showed them the wounds the men made when they killed Him, and He told them, 'Don't be afraid. I'm alive.' Mother told me the story one night."

"Show me," said Lela, nearly falling out of bed in her

eagerness. David found the picture. She gazed long and earnestly at the figure with the lifted hands and at the kneeling, worshiping disciples.

"Don't they look happy," she said at last. "They are not frightened any longer, are they? But I wish He would turn around. Then I could see His face too."

"I don't think anyone knows what His face looked like," said David. "You see, it was a long time ago. Here comes the nurse to take your temperature. I think I'd better go, but I'll come another day and tell you more."

She opened her mouth to beg him to come back, but a thermometer was popped in, so she just smiled and waved.

David sauntered across the compound yard. It was Friday and he had no homework; there would be time to run down to the bay before sunset. He did not want to go with Waffi; he just wanted to go alone with Ragbag who had scampered up the path to meet him. His mind was full of thinking about Lela. If only she could understand about Jesus, her life would be quite different. Jesus would look after her and love her there in her village. She would not need to be lonely or unhappy ever again. He ran faster at the thought of it, bounding down the cliff from tuft to tuft and from rock to rock as lightly as a little goat, with Ragbag barking beside him. Just below stretched the sea, no longer shining and sparkling but muted to a soft gray-blue by the evening. He sang rather breathlessly a chorus he knew as he leaped and skipped:

> Wide, wide as the ocean,
> High as the heaven above,
> Deep, deep as the deepest sea,
> Is my Saviour's love.

Love seemed to be all around him, warming him and mak-

ing him glad in the quiet of the sea under delicate colors
of the sky. He looked across the bay, to the headland where
Lela's village nestled somewhere far back in those folded
hills and valleys. She would be the only one who would
know about the love that was all around each of them. He
stopped skipping and jumping and sat down, leaning back
against a rock, feeling sad for all the villages that had never
heard, for Waffi, for the patients in the hospital who did
not understand. *When I'm big I shall come back and tell
them,* thought David to himself. *I shall be a missionary
like Dad, and perhaps I'll go to those villages and tell them
about Jesus.*

He began daydreaming, letting the warm sand slip idly
through his fingers while staring out over the dusky sea.
He was imagining himself tramping over the hills, a big
strong man like his father, healing the sick and preaching
the gospel, afraid of nobody. He did not realize how dark
it was becoming. Ragbag lay with his nose on his paws and
his eyes half shut. It was such a still evening that even the
ripples only trembled a little on the beach.

Suddenly Ragbag cocked an ear; his body stiffened. He
raised his head and sniffed; then he gave a low growl.
David, startled, took hold of his collar and looked around.
Two men were approaching, and they certainly had not
come around the headland because he would have seen
them, nor had they come down the hill behind, because
they were in front of him. They must have been hiding
down behind the boulders not far from where David was
sitting.

David rolled backward, falling behind the rock, and
flung his arms around Ragbag's neck, imploring him to be
quiet. The dog stopped growling, but his body remained

tensed, as though he knew that these were not ordinary fishermen. David knew too, for they moved fast and purposefully, looking around furtively every few seconds. If it had not been twilight, and if he had not been so small, they would certainly have seen him.

One of them leaped onto the rock that jutted out, dividing the sea from the creek, the creek where David and Waffi had found the little boat. When the man was astride the rock, the other passed him a long object wrapped in a cloth. The first man worked his way along the ridge and then leaned over the edge. Then he came back and took another of those strange long objects. Three or four times he came back and each time he carried yet another one. Then he disappeared over the edge of the rock.

There was silence. Ragbag's whole body was quivering with excitement and the strong conviction that something was going on at which he ought to be barking. But he knew by the presence of the loved hand on his collar that David did not want him to bark, so he kept still.

The second man walked swiftly across to the far side of the bay, looked around the rocks, and came back. He looked up the cliff and all around him but did not see David and Ragbag. Then, having made certain that the coast was clear, he too clung to the crest of the rock and pulled himself along, his bare toes clinging to the slippery crevices and the seaweed. Then he disappeared into the creek. A moment later there was the soft splash of oars, and the boat, like a little gray ghost, glided out into the open sea and disappeared into the dusk.

I suppose they turn the engine on farther out, thought David. His teeth were chattering and he felt very cold. He loosened his grasp on Ragbag and sat up. Everything was perfectly quiet again, so they started up the hill at a run and arrived panting at the top. As he reached the gate he met Waffi who had been looking for him.

"Where have you been?" asked Waffi. "Why have you been running so fast?"

"Down to the bay," gasped David. "I saw the little boat sail away. Two men came with long things in sacks and I hid behind a rock. I saw everything. They didn't turn the engine on. They rowed softly with oars."

Waffi's face darkened. He was terribly jealous that David had this adventure alone and at first pretended not to believe it. They started quarreling and David suddenly turned away shouting, "All right, I'll tell my father about it! He'll believe me."

But Waffi, who really believed every word of it, ran after David and seized him. To get this into the hands of grown-ups was the last thing he wanted, and David's father was the worst sort of parent to know about it. David's parents cared about what he did and might ask questions, and David was always stupid enough to tell them the truth. They might even stop them from playing in the bay. Waffi felt sorry for David. He vastly preferred his own parents who felt that what the eye didn't see the heart could not grieve over. They would never waste time asking him questions.

"David," he whispered hoarsely, "don't tell anyone at all—not a soul. This is our secret, yours and mine, and we'll find out about it all by ourselves. Grown-ups will tell the police, and we won't ever be allowed to play there again."

David hesitated. He was not sure that he wanted to play there again, but on the other hand it was a wonderful adventure, almost as good as a Hardy Brothers mystery. Murray would be green with envy when he heard about it.

"Swear to me," said Waffi, his eyes very big and bright. "If you tell, you'll spoil all the fun. Promise, David, you won't tell."

"All right," said David. He really preferred secrets and adventures that he could share with Mother at bedtime, but after all there was nothing wrong in keeping it to themselves, and it did seem rather brave and manly to have a secret no grown-up in the world knew about. He turned away from Waffi and went home, chewing a nasturtium leaf thoughtfully. Perhaps he could talk to Dad about it in a general sort of way without breaking his promise.

"Dad," he said suddenly at the end of supper, "why do people go out in little boats at night?"

"Fishing," said Dad, whose mind was on a patient with perforated appendix up in the hospital. "Most of the fishing's done at night. The fish can't see the net in the dark."

"Well," said David carefully, "are you allowed to go out in little boats from the bay at the bottom?"

"It's unusual," said Dad. "It's too shallow around there for fish. But I suppose they might pull in. Darling, I shall be late, so don't wait up. Good night, Davie and Joan. You'll be asleep when I get in."

He kissed them hastily and went off. David sipped his milk thoughtfully.

"Mother," he said at last, "if you saw someone carrying long things to a boat when it was nearly dark, what would you think they were?"

"Fishing rods, I suppose," said Mother, who was worrying because Dad had been working late so many nights lately. "Did you see some?"

"Well, yes," said David cautiously, wondering how much further he could go, and keep his promise. "Why would a little boat sail away, just rowing softly, when it had a proper motor?"

"So as not to scare the fish, I should think," said Mother. "Joan, stop licking your fingers and come and have your bath."

David sighed and frowned over his mug. What one-track minds grown-ups had, and how dull they could be at times! He suddenly felt rather lonely and cross. He had risked his life that night and was guarding a tremendous, exciting secret which might be of national importance; and all anyone could think about was fish, fish, fish! If only he could tell them what had happened, how tremendously impressed they would be! If they would just get curious and ask some questions, he would have to tell them a little.

"Mother," he said, following her into the bathroom where she was scrubbing Joan's knees. "Just supposing little boats sail away without any lights—Why do you think a boat would sail away without light?"

"Because of the sardines, I suppose," she answered.

Fish again! thought David.

CHAPTER 5

The Way Home

THE LITTLE BEACH saw less of the boys after David's adventure, for several reasons.

First of all, both were secretly afraid of being there after sunset. They went on a bright Saturday morning and built a dugout of stones and sand into which they decided to creep every evening. The strange thing was, however, that as soon as the light began to soften over the sea and the distances grew misty, one or the other would always remember an urgent appointment which made it impossible to go down to the beach just then, although of course he would be quite free tomorrow. But tomorrow followed tomorrow and the waves lapped each evening on a deserted little shore. From over the fence once or twice they caught sight of a man pacing about on the sand, but they never saw the little boat set off on its secret journey nor, although David often woke before dawn, did they ever see it return.

Second, the weather changed and the winds came sweeping in from the ocean. The sea was a rainy gray, and white-crested waves broke on the beach, tossing their spray over the rock. They could not have climbed along the little creek if they had tried.

Third, Christmas was coming and, although Waffi did

not keep Christmas, David's head was full of it, and his cupboard was becoming full of secrets. He and Dad were making a bookcase for Mother, and although she must have heard plenty of hammering and sawing, she never happened to look out of the window or asked questions, which David thought was quite remarkable. He also had Scotch tape with a dispenser for Dad, a ball for Waffi, and for Joan he had a little doll which he had bought with his own pocket money. He was also making a special album of Bible pictures for Lela in the hospital. He had been to see her every week, taking a picture with him to tell her about the story: but she did not know that they were all being posted in a book for her to take home. That was a surprise.

It would be a Christmas with a big hole in it because it was the first one without Murray; but David was beginning to get used to that, although Mother and Dad were not. He had a tiny Christmas tree which he decked afresh with all the beautiful treasures stored from last year: the silver star, the string of tinsel, and the tiny colored balls. On Christmas Eve he would stand it in the window of the house and everyone would see the lights shining, even the ships out at sea if they glanced toward shore.

The special day dawned clear and blue, the first fine day for a week. The sea was still rough but it sparkled as it tossed, and the sun caught the spray like silver fountains over the rocks. There was no holly or mistletoe, but they shook the rain from the mimosa tree and filled the house with scented, golden boughs, and an old patient from the hospital arrived early with bunches of early wild narcissus. David and Joan opened their stockings in the light of the wild red sunrise over the sea, and then ran out into the new, glistening, sunny, windy world to join the nurses who were singing carols at the door of the hospital. They were singing in the language of the land and David joined them, singing heartily while Joan made loud noises in no language at all, and Ragbag barked. Whatever the effect, everyone was very happy, and Waffi, who sensed presents and food, turned up too.

> Hail, the heaven-born Prince of Peace!
> Hail, the Sun of Righteousness!
> Light and life to all He brings,
> Risen with healing in His wings.

David looked out across the sea where the golden light of the winter sunrise danced on the waves. Sometimes the clouds really did look like great, bright wings spread over the island and the headland—but the carol was talking about Jesus and what happened when He came into a dark, sad heart. David knew all about it this year, so it was the best Christmas yet, in spite of missing Murray.

After breakfast they opened their presents and then went to church, which was more exciting than usual as everyone liked to come together at Christmas to sing the carols in their different languages. But as soon as church was over, David took his precious book and ran over to the hospital to visit Lela.

He found her dressed and sitting in a chair on the sun porch in the sunshine. Each week she looked healthier and happier, and the twisted, bedraggled, monkeylike child who had been carried in three months before was now a pretty, bright-eyed little girl, almost ready to go home again. She was still hunchbacked, but now that she was strong enough to stand straight it showed much less. She greeted him joyfully, thinking he had come to show her

another picture, but when she saw the book she was almost speechless with delight.

"This is even a better book than the last one!" she said when she had turned the pages slowly from start to finish. "The other was all mixed up; there were cats and dogs and houses, just two Jesus pictures at the end. But this is all Jesus pictures and stories. David, you must tell them all over again before I go home. I think I'm going next week, so you must hurry."

She spoke quite calmly and David was surprised.

"Don't you mind going home anymore?" he asked.

"Not as much as I did," answered Lela.

"Why?" enquired David. "Has your master been to see you? Has he been kinder?"

"Oh no," said Lela almost carelessly, "he won't be kinder. I'm not theirs, so why should they be kind? But they want me badly. My mistress has had another baby and she is weak and ill. She says she cannot carry the new baby and turn the grindstone all alone. Besides, the feast is coming near, and who is to whitewash the house for them? They have been three times to ask the doctor to let me go."

"I wish you could stay," said David with a sigh. "It sounds awful in the village."

"It was awful in the village," said the child thoughtfully. "After my mother died, I cried myself to sleep many, many nights. But it won't be so terrible anymore. I know Jesus now. I talk to Him. I know He is with me; He loves me, and if I get sick again and die, like I almost did before I came here, I won't be afraid anymore. I'll just go where He is."

"Were you afraid before?" asked David.

"Of course," said Lela. "I didn't know where I was going. I didn't know what God was like. I knew I was bad, but no one ever told me about Jesus who forgives sins and takes us to His home where we will be happy. You should come and tell all the people who are so lonely in life and so afraid of death."

"Perhaps you can tell them," said David. "Perhaps you'll be like my special verse—shining like a light in the world."

She shook her head rather sadly. "They won't listen to me," she said. "I'm only a little servant girl."

"But Mother said that shining in the world doesn't mean just talking," said David eagerly. "It means being good and showing what Jesus was like. It means speaking the truth when other people tell lies, and being kind when other people are mean and nasty. It means being different, like a light is different from the dark."

"Maybe I can do that," said Lela thoughtfully. "Now tell me the stories, David."

He told her the Christmas story from beginning to end, about the great light that shone on the shepherds and about the Wise Men who followed the star and thought that they were going to a king's palace and were led to a little house instead.

"Weren't they sorry it wasn't a palace?" asked Lela.

"I don't think they minded much," answered David. "It says 'they rejoiced with exceeding great joy' even though they did find just a tiny house. I expect it was like one of your houses in the village, Lela."

"I don't suppose they cared where they were once they had found Jesus. That's how I feel about going home now."

They were silent a moment. Then David suddenly realized that it was time for his Christmas dinner and said good-bye in rather a hurry. They were having a real feast at one o'clock. They had invited four or five lonely Christians and their babies in from the villages, men and women who had heard the gospel in the hospital, had believed, and then had gone back home. None of them could read, so they walked the miles over the mountains hungry and thirsty for more than Christmas dinner. They had all arrived when David came rushing in. Mother was serving up the food on two great dishes, one for the men and one for the women. It was David's favorite dinner, a dish consisting of steamed semolina and flour built up like a sand castle with a nest of onions and raisins and almonds and meat at the top. They all sat on cushions around two low tables and ate out of the two dishes, tunneling into the semolina castle with spoons. Then they had oranges cut in thin slices, sprinkled with sugar and cinnamon, and glasses of sweet mint tea. The villagers talked about their crops and cattle, and their children. Waffi came and peeped in at the window and got himself invited in for cookies and a glass of mint tea.

Then Mother went to the piano, and with shining, joyful faces the guests gathered around and chose the hymns they had learned in the hospital. They had forgotten some of the words and longed to be reminded of them again, for they had nothing else back in the mountains: only the hymns about the Cross and the home in heaven. They longed to learn to read, but it could not be. No one had time to go so far to teach them, so they laboriously learned the verses by heart whenever they came from their villages.

Waffi did not like hymns and was impatient to be off to play with his ball; so he and David soon slipped away into the garden, while Joan went to put her new doll to sleep. David wanted to show Waffi his Christmas presents: the kite Dad had made and was going to fly with them on the cliff; the knife with two blades and a corkscrew and a glass cutter from Mother, and a homemade slingshot which Murray had sent to him. Waffi was fascinated with the slingshot. He had never seen one before and his fingers itched to be pelting stones in all directions.

They played in the garden for a long time and then wandered up to the road with Ragbag, very full and sleepy after his Christmas dinner, waddling contentedly behind them. The road was empty except for the hospital ambulance which stood parked outside the big gates.

"Give me the slingshot," said Waffi excitedly. "I'm going to aim at that tree."

"All right," agreed David. "I'll have a turn after you. We'll see who can hit that low branch leaning down to the road."

But neither was much good at aiming and the stones flew far and wide. Ragbag curled up in the sun on the steps and went to sleep. Waffi narrowly missed a hospital window.

"I don't think we ought to play here," said David uneasily. "It's almost the same as throwing stones with our hands, and we aren't allowed to do that. I'm going to have one more shot at the tree, and then let's go and shoot over the back fence."

He stretched the elastic back as far as it would go and took careful aim, but he must have drawn it askew. The stone, which was quite a large one, whizzed through the air in the wrong direction. There was a sudden crash and the sound of splintering as the ambulance window cracked from corner to corner and little pieces of glass shivered onto the pavement from the hole in the middle. David stood transfixed with horror, staring at the damage. Ragbag woke up suddenly, leaped to attention, and growled menacingly, not quite knowing what was happening, but wanting to be ready.

Waffi alone acted instantly. He snatched the slingshot from David's hand and thrust it into his own ragged pocket. "Quick," he said, seizing David's sleeve and dragging him inside the gate. "No one has seen. No one even knows that we are up here. Come down by the back way and pretend we were playing in the garden all the time.

Your Dad won't think of the slingshot. If he asks you, say
we never even went in the street."

David stood stock-still inside the gate while Waffi tugged
eagerly at his hand. He wanted to think.

"Hurry up, David," pleaded Waffi. "Someone may see
us here. Come with me, quick."

David shook himself free and sat down on a low wall.
His face was very red and he looked very obstinate.

"I'm not coming," he blurted out. "I'm going straight
home to tell Dad."

"To—tell—your—father!" gasped Waffi, who just couldn't
believe his own ears. "What for? Are you out of your
mind? He'll take your slingshot away."

"I don't care if he does," said David, kicking at the grav-
el. "I'm going home to tell him."

Waffi advanced with clenched fists. He could soon bully
David out of this madness, he felt sure. Waffi liked that
slingshot better than any toy he had ever played with, and
he was determined not to lose it.

"If you tell your father," he threatened, "I won't play
with you ever again. You're just a baby. I'll go and play
with the big boys."

"All right!" shouted David desperately. "Go and play
with the big boys. I wish you would. You always try to
make me do bad things and tell lies and steal. I'm not going to do them anymore. It's no good trying any longer
'cause I'm never going to listen to you again. I'm not going
to be a bad boy like you any longer. I'm going to be good."

If he had thrown a bucket of cold water in Waffi's face,
Waffi could not have been more surprised. He stood quite
still, staring, uncertain what to say next. Whatever happened he must not lose David, for, in spite of all his fine

boasting, no big boy ever wanted to play with him. Besides, he liked David better than any other boy he knew. He thought it was far better to lose the slingshot than to lose David. He decided to change his tactics.

"Oh, all right," he said warily. "I didn't want your father to be cross and to take away your slingshot. My father would beat me till he nearly killed me if I broke a window. I have to tell him lies. But if you want to be good, I don't mind, David. Let's still be friends. I'll try to be good too."

"You can't be good by yourself," said David. "I always did naughty things when you told me to until about a month ago. But then I became a Christian, and Christians have to be different, like lights in the dark. Waffi, I wish you'd be a Christian too."

Waffi shook his head. "I follow my father's religion," he said. "He would not let me change." And to himself he added, *I don't want to change either. How could I live, if I had to speak the truth?*

They stood silent. Both were conscious of a gap between them, and they longed to bridge it. *I wish Waffi was a Christian,* thought David. *Then we could both be lights in the dark.*

I wish he didn't care about being truthful and good, thought Waffi. *We could have more fun together if he'd be like me.*

"I'm going home," said David aloud. "It will be time for our Christmas party. He rose to his feet but he did not move. "Come too," he said to Waffi.

"Not if you are going to tell your father," said Waffi cautiously.

"I won't," said David. "Not till the visitors have gone and we're alone."

They went down the path together, both feeling rather sad because both knew now that the other was different and things could never be quite the same again; for it was not a difference you could forget or patch up. Unless one of them changed, the difference had come to stay. It was no good pretending that light and darkness could ever be alike.

But they enjoyed the Christmas party and the guests happily stayed, chatting and singing, until one of the nurses came to take them to the Christmas service in the ward. David went too, to sing and watch the picture slides of the Christmas story.

After it was all over, and the guests had said good-bye, David went home alone. It was a dark night for the moon had not risen. As he turned the corner he looked up and there was his own little Christmas tree with all the candles lit. Its light shone on the dark path, showing him the way home.

He must find Dad at once and tell him about the accident, and the bravely twinkling tree gave him courage. He remembered poor Waffi, creeping along in the dark, always hiding and lying and deceiving and being afraid. He was going to pray for Waffi every night when he said his prayers with Mother, and for himself too, that he might somehow be like that little Christmas tree. For perhaps only by the light of his own courage and truth and kindness would Waffi ever find the way home.

CHAPTER 6

When the Sun Went Down

THERE WERE STILL TEN VACATION days left. Christmas was over and David and Waffi turned their thoughts to the beach once more.

The cold, rainy season had changed to the bright spring, which came early in the year to this land. The days were sparkling cold and clear in the mornings, but hot at mid-day. One afternoon Mother took the children and Lela for a ride in the car and stopped at the foot of a rather boggy hillside where clumps of white jonquils followed a winding stream among the rushes. The children hurriedly pulled off their shoes and socks and waded ankle-deep in the water, picking bunches and bunches of the jonquils for the hospital wards. The air was heavy with the fragrance, announcing that spring was certainly on the way. In a week or two, blue iris spikes would be pushing up in the fields and the almond trees would blossom. Joan, squelching her bare toes in the black mud and sniffing her flowers, felt delightfully happy. And when a little black lamb farther up the hill suddenly did a leap in the air, she tried to do the same, and started frolicking about on the bank on her short, fat legs. The lamb, astonished, scampered off to its mother. Lela laughed till the tears ran down her cheeks, for she had never before seen such a chubby little girl pretending to be a lamb.

David was happy too. The mornings were beginning to get lighter, and he woke every day to flaming sunrises over the sea. He awakened extra early one morning because Ragbag, sleeping beside his bed, seemed to be having a nightmare and had begun leaping up in his basket and growling at a fierce enemy who wasn't there. David turned over sleepily and tickled his ears to keep him quiet. Then he noticed the sky and quite forgot about being sleepy. Instead, he sat up and leaned his arms on the windowsill to watch.

The coast across the water with its white beaches and little towns looked very near, and the mountains behind stood out dark and distinct against the tremendous orange glow that heralded the morning. The sea was still dark but shot with gold reflections. The dawn gradually brightened over the island. David watched and felt that this day was going to be a special one. He would read some verses in his Bible, then get up.

It was a special story that morning, one of his favorites, and he wished he could run up to the hospital and make sure that Lela knew it too; but she had already gone home to her village. It was the story in Matthew 14 of how Jesus walked on the water and Peter tried to walk too. David could understand Peter trying on a morning like this, when every wave was tipped with gold and crimson; but it hadn't been a morning like this for Peter. It had been in the middle of a stormy night—before dawn—with angry tossing waves and not a star to be seen in the sky. How glad Peter must have been when he felt the strong hands of Jesus holding him up.

David thought about the sea and the joy it was to him. Today he would find Waffi and they would go down to the sea, for today was a day for conquest and adventure. Perhaps they could solve the mystery of the little boat. Ragbag could smell adventure too, for he was quivering and sniffing with his paws on the windowsill. David opened the window wider, and the little dog shot out into the dewy garden and went running frantically around the lawn.

David dressed quickly. His mind was full of thinking about the sea and the little boat and the glorious sunny hours that stretched empty before him. He hurried quietly through the living room where Dad was sitting and reading. Mother and Joan were still asleep, and Waffi never got up till about eight. He ran into the cool, sun-drenched world to look for Ragbag and raced happily around the garden with him till breakfast time.

In the end it was afternoon before David found Waffi, for a crowd of visitors came to call on Mother and she asked him to stay and play with Joan while she sat with them and talked and read to them.

The children built a house in the back garden and made it into a store. Joan spread out mimosa balls and pebbles and tiny fir cones and the blue fruits from the eucalyptus trees on large, flat nasturtium leaves; and David was all the different customers, one by one. First he was the old cobbler whose eyesight was so bad that he had to put his nose right into everything he wanted to buy. Then he was the fat butcher, so stuffed with pillows he could hardly get into the shop. Then he was Lady Montague who lived at the Embassy, tripping in on high heels with her Pekingese and a servant behind her to carry her purchases. Joan was delighted and laughed happily, teasing for more, which so encouraged David that he went on thinking of different people to imitate till it was time for dinner.

"You're a good boy, keeping Joan so happy," said Mother gratefully when they came dashing into the house, still laughing over their game.

After dinner, Joan went to sleep and David was free. He ran to the fence and looked down the slope. The sea was rippling and sparkling in the spring sunshine. The tide was low and the beach deserted. Not a single footprint disturbed the pale gold stretch of washed sand. He suddenly felt that he could not wait a minute longer. He tiptoed past Ragbag who was asleep on the step, and then went charging up the path in search of Waffi. Ragbag, they had decided, was rather dangerous on the beach. When the great day came to solve the mystery of the little boat, everything might depend on their lying low and remaining unseen. Ragbag's panting excitement in the face of danger would not help at all.

David met Waffi coming to look for him, and, because it was a bright, clear afternoon filled with ordinary noises, they both felt extremely bold. It was nearly three weeks since they had been to the beach and it was just the right sort of day for brave new beginnings . They looked at each other with shining eyes and started for the beach with silent consent. Both knew that something was going to happen, and both felt ready for it.

They rebuilt their dugout with stones and sand, for the storms had flooded it and carried away its fortifications. While they worked they talked in whispers, for it made them feel mysterious and secret. And all the time they worked they kept their eyes glued to the near headland around which anyone entering the bay must come, unless they came straight down the cliff as Waffi and David had done.

Meanwhile the sun had been moving farther to the West and the hour was getting nearer when something might happen. Already the light was changing to that last clear glow that illumines every detail before it fades. Waffi crept close to David.

"One build, and one keep watch," he whispered. "If they are coming they'll come soon."

He crouched behind a large stone. David went on clearing out their ditch, working as fast as he could. His hands were quite sore with so much scraping and burrowing, but he was well satisfied with the result. No one passing could see them once they snuggled down inside.

Then suddenly Waffi made a queer warning noise and darted back into the dugout, pulling David in beside him backward by the seat of his pants, and they crouched in the wet, sandy burrow clinging to each other with beating hearts.

"Look," breathed Waffi. "They're coming!"

Two swarthy men came around the headland, and passed close in front of them. They were arguing fiercely and both carried long objects under their tattered coats.

"I say, start as soon as it's dark," said one.

"And I say we have time to go back to the town and fetch the others," said the second.

"You're a fool," said the first. "We'll be late. All may be lost if we don't meet the messenger before dawn."

"Well, I'd like to finish the business tonight," replied the other. "It's a full moon, and we're going to do it. I'd like to make this my last trip and go home with the money. I'm tired of this dangerous work."

They stood with their backs to the children, muttering angrily. Then they moved on, still arguing, and began pulling themselves along the side of the rock, hand over hand along the crest. Whatever they carried was bound tightly to their bodies and needed no holding. One disappeared into the creek and the other handed him some long, dark objects. Several minutes later they had started their journey back, and once more they passed in front of the dugout.

"Very well," said one angrily, "as you please! But if we are gone longer than half an hour, I'm not going. By dawn the coast guard may be watching and the messenger will not wait."

"Oh, we'll be back in half an hour," said the other soothingly. "Don't be afraid, my brother. Before the moon is up we'll be off. Let's get going."

They passed on, walking fast. After a time Waffi lifted his head cautiously, and peeped over the side of the dugout. He could see the two figures just going around the headland and a moment later they disappeared.

David and Waffi exchanged a long look. It was much less frightening being two than one. David felt quite brave.

"Half an hour," said Waffi rather breathlessly. "We've got lots of time. We can creep along the top and see what they are. We'll be home before they can come back. It wouldn't take us five minutes."

David hesitated. His heart was bumping very uncomfortably against his ribs; but this was their chance and he mustn't be a coward. He nodded, and they crept cautiously out of their burrow and looked all around them. It was very quiet. The light was fading now and they could not see very far. David felt thankful for the dusk. He would not have dared to venture toward the little boat in the clear sunset glow. But in this dimness, surely it would be safe. Even if the men came back around the headland sooner than expected, the boys would see them in good time to make their escape up the cliff and home over the back fence.

They tiptoed across the sand and scrambled up onto the crest of the rock. Waffi went ahead and David followed. Waffi reached the top of the rock first and peeped over into the boat.

"What is it? Quick!" urged David.

"Nothing," answered Waffi. "The boat's empty—unless —David, maybe there's something under the floorboards. It looks like a high floor."

"Let me see," said David, peering over his shoulder. "They must have hidden those long things somewhere. Maybe that boat does have a false bottom."

"I'm going to get in and look," said Waffi boldly. "You keep watch, David. Can you see the headland?"

"Yes—" answered David doubtfully. "Just. But it's getting dark fast. Waffi, don't be long."

Waffi slipped down into the boat with a small thud and began feeling swiftly around the edges of the floorboards. One was loose and he lifted it with a little squeak of excitement. It was quite light enough to see what lay beneath—a neat stack of guns laid butt to gun barrel.

"They're taking them down to the frontier. It's for the war, David," breathed Waffi, triumph surging up in his young heart. "David, we can't tell. We are on their side. Can you still see the headland?"

"Just," said David uneasily, peering through the gloom. "But come on up now—quick, Waffi; it's getting—Oh!"

Whoever it was who gave him a sharp rap on the head and pinioned his arms behind him had come very softly along the other side of the cliff while David's eyes had been searching the headland.

It was no use struggling, for the strong hand held him as in a vise, and a moment later a swarthy, bearded face peered over David's head and saw Waffi standing in the boat, the raised floorboard in his hands.

"So," said the man with terrible quietness. "You thought there were only two, and you thought they had gone away. But we do not leave our guns unguarded. There is always a third, and he, too, has a gun. Get down into the boat, you European, and sit there with your arms crossed. If either of you move, I'll shoot."

He lowered David into the boat by his arm and the collar of his shirt and sat him down, facing the sea. Neither boy dared to look up. David sat so still that his muscles ached, but he was far too frightened to move so much as a finger. He looked across at Waffi, who also sat like a statue, his face white as chalk against the gray dusk. The walls of the creek shut out the friendly shore lights, and the strip of sky above the sea grew darker and darker. But as David sat staring at it, half senseless and paralyzed with fear, he noticed one thing. One star was shining over the harbor, clear and lonely, like the star on his Christmas tree.

And ever after, when the terror and darkness had all passed away like a bad dream, David could remember that star.

CHAPTER 7

Silver Track on the Sea

THE BOYS DID NOT KNOW how long they sat in that boat. It might have been minutes or hours, for they had lost all sense of time. They only knew that the night was growing darker and darker, and they were growing colder and colder. David's foot went to sleep, but he dared not rub it. Nor did he dare to think of the kitchen light shining out onto the cliff behind him, nor of Dad, who was probably out looking for him by this time; nor of Mother with her warm arms, who would now be thinking that he was late and naughty. The tears brimmed over silently and ran down his cheeks, but he dared not lift his hand to wipe them away.

He thought it must be nearly morning, but actually they had only been there about half an hour when they heard the sound of quick footsteps on the pebbles and a little splash of water as the men waded out toward the ledge in the rock. There was the sound of a sharp, frightened question; an answer, the words of which they could not hear, and then the sound of scuffling and, although they still dared not look up or move, they knew that three faces were watching them.

"Well," said the first voice very quietly, "what are you going to do with them?"

"Take them out to where the water is deep," said the second voice. "If they have seen what there is to see, they must not go home again. You can't trust children. The coast guard would be waiting for us at the other side, and it would be prison for all of us."

"Be careful," said the deep voice of the man who had caught them. "One of them is a European child."

"All the worse!" said the second. "He's probably French, and they will be down to look for him in no time. We'd better get moving. Guard those children with your gun. They might try to escape where it is shallow."

The little craft lurched against the creekbank as its owner let himself down into it, followed immediately by the second man. A moment later David felt his arms secured firmly with a rope, and he was lifted up, helpless, and then tied to the back seat. The other man stepped swiftly across and did the same to Waffi, and two rags were tied firmly around their mouths. It was all a matter of seconds, so quickly and purposefully did the men move, and when David came to his senses again the boat was out of the creek, and the two men were rowing swiftly and silently, their oars making practically no sound as they struck the water.

They rowed for about ten minutes and then leaned toward the control panel in the prow. A quiet *chug-chug* started up, and the boat began to move fast, kicking a little at the throbbing of the engines. The first man got up and stepped over to the boys in the back of the boat and cut the rags from their mouths. Waffi burst into hysterical screams; but it did not matter now. They were too far from the shore for anyone to hear, and they were getting out into the deep waters.

David did not scream because it did not seem to help; but he turned his head to look at the top of the cliff far behind them. He thought it must be nearly the middle of the night but the lights were still shining. Of course they were, thought David, for Mother and Dad would never go to bed without him. Only Joan would be lying asleep in her cot, rosy and curly, her doll clasped in her arm. He had never known before how much he loved Joan. He dared not think too hard about his parents lest his heart should break.

His neck was too strained to look backward any longer, so he turned his head and blinked in surprise, for the water ahead was no longer gray, but silver. The moon had risen, making a silver track of light across the sea, just as it had done on the night when he had become a true son of God. He suddenly remembered the story he read that morning. "It is I; be not afraid," said Jesus to poor frightened Peter, and Peter had probably stepped down from the boat and walked along the shining pathway leading straight from him to the feet of Jesus. Perhaps that silver track was now God's way of reminding him that Jesus was still close beside him on that lonely sea, reaching out His hand to him, loving him, keeping him.

"Waffi," he whispered, "I am going to pray."

Waffi, finding that no one took the slightest notice, had stopped screaming, and was huddled, exhausted, on the seat with his head resting on David's shoulder, his body shaken with quiet sobbing. Yet he had wondered, in the midst of his terror, at David's controlled stillness. Did David really believe that his God could save them? Was there some power, known only to Christians, that could help them now? Waffi felt he would willingly try anything if only he knew how. He wriggled as close as he could to David. The pressure of their cold little bodies comforted them.

"Who are you?" asked the taller man, turning to them suddenly. "You, son of our country, what is your father?"

"A tr-truck driver," whispered Waffi through chattering teeth. The shore lights were all left behind now, and the water looked very, very deep.

"And you, the French boy," rapped out the man. "Who is your father and where do you live?"

He spoke in French and David stared at him blankly. "I don't understand; I am English," he replied in the man's native language.

The man peered at him curiously. "English, and he speaks with our tongue!" he exclaimed. "Who are you?"

"I'm the son of the doctor at the English hospital," answered David, and at the thought of his kind, strong father his voice trembled. But the man had come very close to him and was staring hard at the little white face lifted to his in the moonlight.

"The English doctor's son?" repeated the man. "The tall doctor with the little scar on his forehead?"

"Yes," answered David, and this time he gave a little sob. The man sat down quite close to him, still staring and stroking his beard. Suddenly he turned to his friend who was steering the ship.

"That doctor is a faithful man," he said, "and a father to the poor. When I was a boy my parents died and no one dressed the sores on my leg. He found me and took me in. I was months in that hospital, and he dressed my wounds with his own hands. Without him I should have been a lame beggar. I will not harm one hair of his son's head. We must think of some other plan."

"There is no other plan," cried his friend in alarm. "If those children reach home we are lost."

"No, we are not," replied the first, who seemed to be working something out. "Listen to me. In the dark hour before the dawn we shall pass the next headland. We will sail in at the foot of the cliff and leave the children on the beach at the bottom of the path. Within the hour we will hand over the guns and receive the money and that's enough for me. The children will walk for some hours before they find a village, and then they will sleep. The hillmen and their donkeys do not move fast. It may be sunset tonight, or even tomorrow, before they will return them to their parents. At dawn we can hide the boat and the guns will be up in the high mountains long before nightfall. The tribesmen have their own paths to the frontier and they do not give away secrets."

The other man seemed troubled and angry. A long whispered argument followed and the little boat throbbed on through the deep, deep, water.

Suddenly the first speaker turned back and looked at the boys.

"I'm not afraid of that one," he said pointing at Waffi. "He is a son of our country, and our war is his war. His people will not betray us. It is the other one I fear. And yet, for his father's sake, I will not harm him."

He leaned over till his face was very close to David's.

"Listen, little one," he said. "We will take you safe to land, and when you reach home, tell your father all that happened. Tell him he was merciful to me when I was a child, and I have been merciful to his child. And tell him, for the love he bears toward the people and the land, not to betray us."

"I'll remember," said David solemnly. "And I'll explain to my father that we mustn't tell."

He was shivering with cold and dizzy with sleep and strain, but he was no longer afraid. This man was kind, and somehow, some day, they would reach home again.

The man got up suddenly, took a knife from his pocket and cut the cords that bound the children. He laid them down gently between the seats and covered them with an old piece of sailcloth. The boards were hard and the night air was cold, but the sea rocked them gently, and the splash of the silver water on the prow soothed them like a lullaby. The moon had swung clear of the horizon, and David looked up into its pure bright face. The light seemed to wrap him in a shining peace, as though strong, loving arms were holding him fast. He flung his own arm across poor frightened little Waffi as though to draw him closer to his own comfort.

I wish Waffi knew, he thought to himself. *Oh, I wish he knew!* And then everything faded, and he slept as deeply and soundly as if he were in his bed at home. And the stars in their settings shone above him, and the moon moved in its course toward the black summits of the mountains. The dark hour before the dawn was drawing near, and the little craft with its precious burden turned inland toward the lovely beaches of the hill country.

CHAPTER 8

Safely Led

D<small>AVID WOKE WITH A START</small> and not
the slightest idea where he was. He was cold and stiff and
lying on bare, wet boards. A large hand was shaking him
urgently but not unkindly. All around him were strange,
unfamiliar sounds: the grating of the keel on a pebbly
shore, the slapping of waves against the side of the boat,
the sighing of wind on black water, and the whispering of
men's voices.

David began to cry with cold and bewilderment and the
shadow of some half-remembered terror. But a hand was
clasped firmly over his mouth till he stopped, and then he
was lifted in strong arms that smelled of gasoline and tobacco and set down on his feet on the pebbly beach. So
dizzy was he with sleep and bewilderment that he fell over
sideways, but the man picked him up again and propped
him against a rock. A moment later Waffi was dumped beside him, and they huddled gratefully together.

"I must leave you," whispered the man. "The path up
the cliff is just behind you, but you must wait till it gets
light. It's not an hour now till dawn. Follow that path
across the hills till you come to a village. It's a long way
but you can't miss it. Tell them who you are, and they
will take you home. Your father is loved by the hill people.

Go in peace, and may God help you. Don't forget my message."

He was gone, and they heard the prow grate on the pebbles as the little boat moved away from the shore, and then the noise of the engine which died away in the darkness. It was very dark indeed now; the moon had set but the inky sky was crowded with fierce bright stars, blazing their last before their light faded. The cliff loomed behind them black and threatening, and just to their right a little stream splashed down a gully into the sea.

It was no good looking for the path just yet. There was nothing to do but to sit and wait, and while they waited David watched the stars. His father had taught him about them, and he tried to find the constellations—Orion's belt, the Pleiades, the Milky Way, and sometimes, behind the mountains, the Southern Cross. Waffi whimpered and sniffed beside him, but David had stopped crying. There was no longer a silver pathway on the water, but surely the One who had walked on the sea and had drawn so near to them would guide them home!

"Ai, ai!" moaned Waffi. "We shall die of cold on this beach before morning comes. Aren't you afraid?"

David was silent. He was terribly afraid of the darkness and the tide and the mountains behind them, but his fear was like the little stream beside them, ever tumbling toward that ocean depth of strength and love, and being lost forever. He could not explain, but he wished Waffi knew.

"I think we shall get home," he answered comfortingly. "And anyhow, they did not throw us into the sea."

"Ah, David, you are brave," sobbed Waffi. "Is it your Jesus who makes you brave?"

"He's looking after us," answered David simply. "Shall I tell you how He walked on the waves, Waffi? It's no good trying to go yet."

"Yes," said Waffi with a tired sigh, and the two little boys snuggled close as they could to each other in the shelter of the rock, while David told his story.

". . . and when Jesus came into the boat everything was quiet and calm and no one was afraid anymore," finished David. "Look, Waffi, the light's beginning to come."

They turned and sat with their faces turned east where the darkness had begun to pale. Already there was no more blackness. The sky was a deep blue, and the starlight was fading. The cliff rose ghostly gray behind them, and they could see the white foam breaking on the gray beach.

"I think we could see the path now," said David. "Let's go and look."

They stretched themselves, trying to get rid of the cold and stiffness, and limped painfully to the foot of the cliff. They soon found what they wanted—the bottom of a stony little track that wound its way up the face of the cliff. They started scrambling, clinging to the tufts of coarse grass and to the tamarisk bushes. The higher they climbed the lighter it grew. By the time they had reached the top, the sea at their feet stretched away, a sheet of silver-blue flecked with crimson, and the island rose from the mist like a fortress against a rosy sky. They sank down on the grass for a moment to rest and watch, but it was cold with dew. They got up and, turning their backs to the brightening East, took stock of the road ahead.

In front of them stretched the hilly uplands seamed with rock, rising higher into the hills and falling into valleys until it met the clear sky. The path seemed to run straight and true although as yet there was no village in sight. They set off, trudging along in silence, for they were very weary; but there were many things along the way to cheer them. The sun rose and was warm on their backs, and they came to a spring where they could drink. Narcissus grew in scented clumps in the marsh where the water flowed, and once they came to a starry field of blue iris, wide open and dew-spangled. But each time they came to the brow of a hill and hoped to see a village, they were disappointed. The barren, uninhabited uplands seem to go on forever.

At last they stumbled to the top of a hill higher than the others, and straight in front of them across the next valley, like a sheer, impassable wall, rose the mountains, their rocks red in the early light.

"We can't climb those!" cried Waffi, in a panicky voice. "There are monkeys and wild boars up there. I think we have lost our way."

"No, we haven't," said David. "He told us to follow the path. Look, Waffi, there, down in the valley, there's a flock of goats, and over there I can see some smoke. I think we have nearly reached the village."

"Praise be to God!" exclaimed Waffi fervently. "Let's go on! Do you think they will give us food, David? I am so hungry and empty I could eat the grass!"

"I think they will," said David, who had never experienced anything but kindness from the people of the land. They trudged on, their feet blistered from the wetness of their sandals and the roughness of the road.

Very soon the stony grassland and the low shrubs gave place to cultivated fields and terraced vineyards and old, gnarled olive trees. The village was built on the slopes of the river basin at the bottom of the valley, and red rocks rose sheer on the other side.

They approached cautiously. A man was ploughing with a rough, wooden plough and a yoke of oxen. He stopped and stared curiously but said nothing. A lean dog ran out and barked at them, but Waffi threw a stone at it and the dog ran away growling. Then they reached a well where a few little girls were filling their buckets and chattering like magpies. They all stopped talking suddenly and gazed in astonishment at the blue-eyed, fair-haired, and dirty-faced boy who suddenly appeared in their midst dragging his blistered feet wearily. Some of them in that remote village had never seen such a person before.

"Who is he?" they whispered after a moment's silence. "Where does he come from?"

"French," said another and laughed rather rudely.

"What has he come for?" said a third in a nervous voice. "Perhaps there are other Frenchmen with him. And that boy there! Who is he? He is not from our village."

They looked fierce and frightened, and David's heart sank. He felt frightened too but not fierce; only unutterably weary and hungry and thirsty. *Oh, God!* he prayed in his heart, *please send someone kind. Please, please take me where I can lie down and go to sleep, and send someone to take us home.*

The children stood looking at each other shyly and uncertainly. Waffi asked for a drink of water, and the little maidens began giggling and whispering among themselves. They spoke the slow dialect of the tribes, and Waffi's town accent struck them as strange and amusing. The boys moved on, and one of the girls threw a handful of small pebbles after them, but even Waffi was too tired to throw anything back.

"Let's go to the river," said David. "We might find some women washing. Little girls are no good!"

They wandered on past a few thatched mud huts where babies played in the doorways. From one came the sound of a grindstone, but no one noticed the two little boys. They could hear the splashing of the river on the stones now, and around the next turn in the path they saw a little beach ahead of them where women and girls squatted with their washing. Charcoal fires burned on the stone, with big boiling kettles steaming on top of them, and the amber water was frothy with soap. Clothes and garments of all shapes and sizes, laid out to dry in the sun, decorated the bank. Still no one noticed the two shy children who stood watching, peeping out from behind an olive tree.

Suddenly David jerked to attention.

A little figure was coming down the path singing softly to herself. She could not see him, for she was carrying a big bundle of washing on her shoulder, shutting out all her view on that side, and he could not see her face. But he could see that her back was hunched and could hear the words she was singing, the words they sang night after night in the hospital wards when the nurse played the small organ and sang with the patients.

> I was lost; but Jesus found me,
> Found His sheep in the desert,
> Carried me back on His shoulders,
> Set my feet in God's way.

"Lela!" David yelled, and he flung himself upon her, scattering her dirty washing far and wide all over the path.

She gave a little shriek of fear and nearly fell backward, for although she was older than he was, she was not much larger.

"It's me, David, the doctor's son," cried David, his face alight with joy, his weariness forgotten. Lela, recognizing him, thought she must be dreaming, and holding him at arm's length, she stared and stared. But all the time she stared her face was growing brighter as it slowly dawned on her understanding that this really was her little friend.

"Ah, David," she said at last; and then she could say no more, for tears of joy and love were rolling down her cheeks. The women had left their washing on the stones and were all crowding around and shouting questions. They were big women with strong brown arms, but David was not afraid of them. He looked up and laughed at them, and they laughed back at his fair hair and blue eyes. Then they saw Waffi and turned on him with a torrent of questions: "Who—?" "Where—?" "Why—?"

Waffi squatted down under the olive tree because he was too tired to stand any longer and told them most of the story, and it lost nothing in the telling. He was particularly careful to inform them that he and David had had nothing to eat since the day before, and they wanted some breakfast, but he remembered their promise and did not mention the guns. The women squatted on the muddy path or stood with their hands on their hips as they listened and uttered exclamations of astonishment. Their voices were loud and their faces were swarthy, but their hearts were very kind, and they all wanted to take the young boys home and feed them; but that honor belonged to Lela. Honors did not often come her way, but David was hers, and hers alone.

"Come," she said importantly, gathering the clothes up

from the mud and tying them in a bundle, "we will go to my mistress." She turned back up the path, and Waffi and David followed her, refreshed by the very thought of food and rest. They soon came to a cactus hedge enclosing a mud house. Two little children played by the step and a woman sat in the doorway kneading bread. David recognized her at once. It was the woman he had met on the cliff the day Lela came into the hospital.

"My mistress," cried Lela, "the doctor's son has come. He and another child have come on foot from the coast. We must feed them, my mistress, and take them home."

The woman rose at once, quite excited at the news, and drew the children into the cool shade of the hut. She thought it was always good to keep "in" with the hospital, for who knew who might be ill next? But she was also a kind woman and was touched by the sight of two such weary, dirty little boys. She spread a rush mat and brought them buttermilk and coarse rye bread. Lela ran behind the house and came back with two brown eggs which she broke into a frying pan. Then she blew on the charcoal under it. At the smell of the sizzling oil the children wriggled and squirmed in joyful anticipation. There were no knives and forks. They ate out of one clay dish, cleaning up the last drop of fat with the bread.

"When can I go home?" asked David, but he was almost too tired to hear the answer, nor did he bother much. He was safe with Lela and she would arrange things somehow. The woman drew the rush mat into a quiet, dark corner, placed a cushion under the boys' heads and covered them with a bright, handwoven rug; and without a "good night" or "thank you," they both dropped into a deep, exhausted sleep.

CHAPTER 9

Only a Little Light

WHEN DAVID WOKE, the sun had already dipped behind the red rocks across the river and the evening was cool and quiet. Waffi was still fast asleep. David felt as though he never wanted to move again, for his limbs were stiff and heavy from the cold sea and the long walk inland. So he just lay still, peeping over the top of the blanket and listening to the clucking of the hens outside, the sound of running water at the bottom of the path, the bubbling from a pot on the charcoal, and the soft chatter of Lela and her mistress. They were sitting in the doorway teasing and combing brown sheepswool and winding it into balls.

"I'm going across to the neighbors to see if they will lend me some nice, fresh mint," said Lela's mistress. "We must have a good meal ready when the doctor comes for his son. He will surely come tonight when he gets the message. You watch the stew, and I'll take the children with me."

She tossed the baby onto her back and went away with the two older children clinging to her dress. Lela only waited till she had disappeared around the cactus hedge before she screwed herself around to look at David who raised his head to smile at her over the top of the blanket. She gathered the wool into her lap and came and sat down beside him on the mat.

"The time is flying, David," she said sadly. "My master went to carry the news to your father as soon as you slept. It is a long walk over the mountains, but they will soon be back for sure, and then you will go. All day I have wanted to wake you, but my mistress would not let me."

"Why did you want to wake me?" asked David. "I was so tired that I don't think I'd have heard you."

"Why?" repeated Lela impatiently. "To tell me more, of course. Just think, David, no one has told me anything or spoken to me about the Lord Jesus since I came back to the village. I look at the picture and I try to remember, but I forget so much. Tell me more, David. Tell me more about Jesus. Tell me how I ought to pray. I want to know so many things, I could listen all night."

"Praying is telling God everything," answered David. "I prayed in the boat."

"And what happened?" asked Lela.

"I remembered how Jesus walked on the sea. There was a shining, moonlight path on the water which looked as though—as though He were coming to me, and I wasn't so afraid after that. Then they told us they weren't going to throw us into the sea, and I knew we were going to be safe. And at the well I prayed I'd find someone kind, and I found you."

"Oh, oh!" cried Lela, wringing her hands, overcome by the thought of the troubles and dangers that her friend had been through. "But the Lord answered your prayers. David, I am going to pray that another Christian will come and teach me more. How can I be a Christian alone? I don't dare to tell anyone. They would beat me. And I have no one to talk to or to teach me."

"I know one way," said David. "You can be different.

When Dad comes I'll ask him to tell you my verse. It's about sons of God shining like lights in the dark because Jesus makes them different. You are the only light in the village now. It means that when everyone else tells lies, you will be truthful, and when everyone else is cross and unkind like those little girls at the well, you will be kind. I'm a Christian, and Waffi isn't, and we are different. After I remembered about Jesus last night, I wasn't really afraid anymore, but Waffi was afraid all the time."

Waffi pricked up his ears. He had been wide awake for the last five minutes but, like David, he had not felt like moving, so he had just lain quietly. The other two children, deep in conversation, had not noticed him. He had not listened much to the first part of their talk, but the last sentence struck him forcibly because it was true. He shut his eyes and pretended to be asleep again. He wanted to think it over.

David was younger than he was, yet he, Waffi, had been almost out of his mind with fear, and David had seemed quiet and calm after the moon came out. Could it be that this Jesus, who David sometimes talked about, could take away the fear of death and darkness? Had there really been Someone there all the time? Someone Waffi did not know, but David did, who had saved and comforted and guided? If so, Waffi wished he knew Him too. He still could not think about that black, lonely ocean without terrible shudders of horror. But David apparently did not remember the horror as much as he remembered the Person who had been there, the Person Waffi did not know. There were so many evil, frightening things in life. Waffi knew much more about them than David did. It would be good to have Someone always close to you to keep you safe and to look after you. One day perhaps, when they were back in the shelter of the garden, he would ask David all about it.

He lay, half thinking, half dreaming, and the other two chatted on. The little hut was almost dark now, but through the open doorway they could see a patch of yellow sky. The air was warm and fragrant with the steam of the partridge stew, and very soon Lela's mistress came back, with her babies toddling behind her, and lighted the lamp. Waffi stopped pretending to be asleep, and they drew the mat up to the fire and gathered around the glowing charcoal; and all the time David was straining his ears for the sound he knew would come soon and for which he felt he could wait no longer.

Just before dark it came. First there was a barking of dogs, then the voices of men; and David shot out of the door and across the mud yard, scattering the hens right and left, and fell into his father's arms just as he appeared through the gap in the prickly pear hedge. His father hugged him and hugged him as though he would never let him go again. Waffi's father was there too, and he pushed them both aside and strode forward to find his own son.

"Dad," whispered David, still holding him tightly, "you won't tell the police about us, will you, or let them ask questions about us? He was a kind man, and we promised."

His father laughed.

"The men were caught this morning, Davie," he said. "Mercifully, Waffi had told his father about that little boat. We knew you had gone to the beach and he guessed you might have gotten mixed up with a gang of gun raiders. By midnight the whole coast was being patrolled and the

roads to the frontier too. The little boat was found in a creek this morning; it must have slipped in before dawn. The guns were found up in the mountains hidden in a truckload of frozen fish, and the men were traced this afternoon. They must be thankful they let you go. Smuggling is a light sentence—harming young boys is not."

"Oh!" said David. He was sorry for the men, yet in one way he felt rather relieved. His secret had been weighing heavily on him and he felt he never wanted to have another secret as long as he lived. He relaxed against his father's shoulder. "Let's go home to Mother," he whispered.

"Soon," said Dad, "but we must stay a little and thank the kind people and Lela. Mother knows you are safe, so we need not be in too great a hurry."

Indeed, it was no good being in too great a hurry, because the tables had already been set, and the feast was being laid. The partridge stew was poured into a clay dish, and the new loaves were broken into hunks. Rugs and mats were spread on the floor, and they all sat down in the steaming little room. The smell of the oil lamp mingled pleasantly with the smell of hot bread and savory meat and fresh mint. The men, each with a little son leaning against him, gathered around, and Lela and her mistress sat a little apart ready to serve, and prepared to brew the tea.

It was a good supper and the hungry children did full justice to it. Everyone talked at once about the extraordinary events of the previous night, except Lela. She sat silent, her hands clasped, her heart as heavy as lead.

David's father had come so suddenly and after supper they would go so quickly. She would not be able to speak to them alone or ask all the questions that were crowding into her mind. She was hungry for the Bread of Life, yearning to know more, but there would be no further chance. Yet David had told her one thing to which she could cling. She would be different, like light in the dark. Jesus could make her different. She did not know how, but David had said He could.

The meal was finished, and the doctor was eager to leave as soon as possible. He rose, thanking his kind host, and Lela glided to his side and looked up into his face, her eyes bright in the lamplight with unshed tears.

"Aren't you going to tell them?" she whispered. "They'll never hear unless you do."

He hesitated. He knew his wife would be getting very anxious, and the rough mountain roads would make driving difficult in the dark. But as he stood looking down into the child's imploring face, there was a rustle and a whispering outside and the sound of bare feet plodding across the mud. A dog barked, a baby began to cry. The feet halted.

"Who's there?" called Lela's master.

There was a moment's tense silence; then the answer came cautiously: "It is the sick of the village. We hear the good doctor is with you."

"Come in," called the host, and they pushed open the wooden door and surged into the room—a weak old man with sores on his legs, a mother carrying a skinny baby with measles, a woman shading her half-blind eyes from the light, and another mother carrying a twisted little cripple. Their faces were bright with hope and trust as they stood displaying their needs and waiting for the doctor to speak.

"Listen!" said David's father. "I have no medicine and I cannot wait. Today is Wednesday. On Saturday I will come back. I will bring my medicine and I will bring the Book that tells the way to heaven. Tell all the sick people to gather at noon. I will come."

"So will I," said David.

"And me," said Waffi.

Lela said nothing. A little servant girl must not appear too eager, but she squeezed her hands together for joy and backed into the shadows behind the corn bin. The people were pleased too.

"Don't forget, don't forget, surely come!" they called after the doctor when, having thanked their host again from the bottoms of their hearts, the visitors at last managed to leave. The moon had risen and the olive trees looked ghostly silver. David and Waffi were tempted to play on the moonlight patterns but their feet were too sore and blistered. They could only hobble.

They were glad to snuggle against their fathers in the warm car and to start the long, bumpy journey home. They drove slowly along an uneven mule track, and there was nothing to see but silver mountains against a starry sky and now and then patches of white narcissus, ghostly white in the moonlight. But after many miles of bumping, they reached a main road. Then Dad got up speed and they went racing through the night, on and on, till they could see the sea on their right and the lights of the town ahead, and David felt as though it was years and years since he had seen Mother. So much had happened to him, inside and out, since the night before, that he felt like a completely new boy. Life, he thought, would never be quite the same again.

He could see the harbor. Then they were climbing the hill. There ahead were the orange windows of the hospital, and Mother and Joan and Ragbag standing under the porch lamp in a circle of light. Dad pulled up beside them, and David flung himself across Waffi's father, accidentally giving him one in the eye as he passed, tumbled out the door, and was swallowed up in Mother's arms while Joan passionately kissed the seat of his trousers, and Ragbag barked and barked and barked. David was home.

CHAPTER 10

The Message of the Stars

AFTER A BATH and a long night's sleep there seemed no particular reason why David should not go back to school as usual; but he found it rather difficult to start life again as though nothing had happened, and he was not particularly easy to live with during the next few days. He had had a bigger shock than he knew, and he was tired and cross and kept wanting to cry when there was nothing to cry about. He teased Joan till she cried too, and his schoolteacher often found him not paying attention to his lessons. By Friday night he was miserable and fed up. He wandered out into the garden and met Waffi.

"Hello," said Waffi. "Want to go down to the beach? It's safe now."

"I'm not allowed to," answered David, scowling. "Not anymore; not without Dad."

"Oh," said Waffi, "let's play in the garden then. Let's play with your bow and arrows."

But Waffi, as usual, wanted the best and tried to snatch the straightest arrow every time, and David was in no mood to lose the game. "You're cheating," said David crossly. "You've got the best bow and the straightest arrow. Trade with me, and I'll win easily."

"I haven't," retorted Waffi. "They're all the same."

"You have! They're not!" shouted David, losing his temper and making a grab at the bow. Waffi hung on, and David pulled. The result was as might be expected. There was a sudden crack and the bow snapped in half.

"You—you—!" shouted David furiously. "You've broken my best bow. You always break my things. I'll never play with you anymore."

"And I don't want to play with you anymore," answered Waffi coolly, flinging his piece lightly into the bamboos and turning scornfully on his heel. "I don't want anything more to do with you—or anything more to do with Christians either! Christians are as selfish and cross as other people. There's no difference."

He walked away up the path rather slowly, half expecting David to run after him, but David had turned away to hide the tears that had started, and was standing by the fence looking out over the sea, a big lump in his throat. So this was the end of his hopes and prayers! He'd prayed so hard Waffi would be a Christian and now it was all spoiled. Waffi would never believe now that Christians were different, and David half wondered if they really were.

He looked down at the broken bow he had made with such care a couple of weeks before. Bows never lasted very long; they always broke sooner or later and then you made another. So had it really been worth getting into such a fight? His gaze wandered over the sea and the gray-blue sky tinged with pink. He had often come to his private little corner under the mimosa tree in the evening to look at the sky, and it was always beautiful at sunset, even when he was cross and bad-tempered. The best things never broke or got spoiled or changed—like the sea or the sunset or the stars or God. Very soon the moon would rise and there would be a silver track across the sea, like on the night when he had been so frightened and he knew Jesus had been with him. Perhaps because Jesus never changed, He would always come when David was in need; perhaps He would come now because David was sorry and longing to be good. Perhaps it was only David himself that kept changing. It was a comforting, steadying thought like finding a rock to stand on when you thought you were being carried out of your depth by a big wave.

"I'm sorry," he whispered, standing very still. The beauty all around him stole in on his sadness and comforted him. A small gull rose up on white wings and flew away into the sunset. A pink feathery cloud drifted above the lighthouse on the far headland. The star that he always saw first was suddenly there, shining in its right place. Nothing was spoiled or broken except the bow which did not matter any longer, and his hopes and prayers for Waffi which could probably be mended if he said he was sorry.

He turned around slowly, because he did not want to say sorry to Waffi. It had been the fault of both of them. He was glad there was nothing to be done about it then. Waffi would certainly have gone home and it might be easier in the morning.

But Waffi had not gone home. He was particularly anxious to be said sorry to, as he wanted to go on the expedition next day, and his pride would make it impossible if he and David were still not on speaking terms. So when, on looking back, he had seen David standing under the mimosa tree he had decided to wait. He knew that standing under the tree and gazing out to sea always had a good effect on David's temper. So as David strolled around the corner of the house, he came face to face with Waffi sitting on the doorstep.

Both little boys surveyed each other cautiously. Then Waffi moved over and made room. After a little hesitation, David accepted the unspoken invitation and sat down beside him. If they squeezed close together there was just room for both on the step.

"Sorry," said David.

"Sorry," said Waffi.

"You can come tomorrow," said David.

"I'll make you another bow," said Waffi.

"I'll let you shoot the straight arrow," replied David.

They sat on in silence thinking how nice it was being friends again. The dusk grew deeper around them and the stars came out one by one. Then David's mother called him in to supper, and Waffi started home for the second time.

But Waffi walked slowly, thinking hard. How quickly David had come back and said sorry! How forgiving he had been about the broken bow! Waffi had quarreled with all the other boys, because he was so selfish and always wanted the best of everything, and it never came out right. They never said sorry, and Waffi just went on feeling angry and unforgiving. If Christians could put things right like that, he would like to be a Christian; for boys could be fierce and cruel when they quarreled. How peaceful it had been sitting on that step together after they had both said sorry.

What did it mean to be a Christian, he wondered. What did you have to do? David could tell him, no doubt, but he was too proud to ask. His father would be very angry if he mentioned such a thing, and he did not dare to go to Sunday school. Then he remembered they were going out to the village next day, and the doctor would read the Book to the people. Perhaps he would tell them how to become Christians, and Waffi would listen hard. If it was a cure for fear and a cure for quarreling, it was worth understanding.

David ate his supper rather quietly, and his mother, who had seen the end of the fight out of the kitchen window, watched him thoughtfully and wondered what he had been thinking about standing there weeping, with his broken bow, under the mimosa tree. Something had happened, for he was no longer the restless, irritable, unreasonable little boy he had been at dinner time. He was particularly good and helpful and cleared the table and swept up the crumbs without being asked.

"I don't know what I'd do without you, David," said Mother gratefully. "You've made the room so nice and tidy. And, do you know, David, I'm going to need your help more than ever soon, because something is going to happen."

"What?" asked David who was riding the broom around the table.

"It's a big secret," said Mother. "When you are in bed I'll tell you."

What is going to happen? thought David as he washed as little of himself as possible and hurried into his pajamas. He ran into the dining room and skipped three times around the table because he was so happy. All the crossness of the last few days had gone like a dream and he was feeling good again. Tomorrow he was going to the village with Dad and Waffi; tonight there was a secret, and he knew it was a nice secret by the way Mother had spoken.

"Are you ready, Mother?" he called, bouncing on his bed.

"Nearly," called back his mother who was tucking in Joan.

"Well hurry up, 'cause I want to know about that thing you told me," shouted David. They mustn't mention the secret to Joan because she wasn't going to be told. She was too small to understand. It was a grown-up secret to be shared between David and Mother.

"You'll break those springs, David," warned Mother. "Get into bed at once."

So he got in, and she came and knelt down beside him, as she always did when there was anything special to tell. And tonight it was very, very special. David could hardly believe it. After Mother had gone away he lay thinking and thinking about it in the dark.

They were going to have a new baby in only two months. When the flowers were out in the fields and the garden was full of white lilies, before it really got hot, before the Easter holidays, the baby would have arrived. It would be his own baby and he would help Mother plan the names. If it was a girl he wanted Rose, because the rosebuds were just coming out in the garden; but if it was a boy he wanted Peter, because Peter had walked on the sea and Jesus had come to him across the waves.

His mother would need him very badly because Joan was scarcely more than a baby, and Dad was out such a lot. She would be in bed at first and then she would feel tired for a time, and even when she was quite well again there would be a lot of extra work: feeding the baby, bathing it, washing its clothes, singing it to sleep. He tried to remember what it was like when Joan was born, but at five years of age he had not felt responsible and had barely noticed what was happening. Now it was different. He felt all ready for this baby.

Then suddenly he remembered, and he clenched his fists under the covers.

He was going away to school only five months after the baby was born, and he would have to leave it behind for a whole year. He had minded before, but now he minded ten times more, and two hot tears trickled down his cheeks.

"Oh, God," he whispered into the darkness, "please let something happen so I don't have to go. I want to be a missionary when I grow up, and I don't need lots of lessons to be a missionary. I could stay here and learn with Dad and help with the new baby. Oh, please don't make me go."

He dried his tears with the sheet and stared out of the window. It was a clear night and every star was shining in its own right place, each lighting its own little patch of darkness. They would stay steadfastly on, in their own appointed places, until their tiny glow would be lost in the breaking of the dawn and the darkness would be scattered.

But David was too young and too sad to understand the message of the stars. He turned away from the window and, burying his face in the pillow, he wept bitterly.

CHAPTER 11

"God Hath Shined in Our Hearts"

Dad, David, and Waffi started three times the next morning before they actually left, because the doctor always found it difficult to escape from the hospital. The telephone rang when they were halfway to the gate and he had to go back and answer it. Then they were stopped by someone who wanted medicine just as they were out into the road. But at last everyone was dealt with, and they swung out of sight around the corner, and the two impatient little boys felt safe at last.

Waffi, with his head stuck far out of the window, was quieter than usual, for he felt that today was going to be a very special day. Perhaps today he would hear some secret that would make him happy and stop his being afraid. He still lay awake every night unable to think of anything but those black waves that had nearly swallowed him up; and when he did go to sleep, he often woke in the grip of a horrible nightmare. If being a Christian could take away fear, he was willing to try it. There was no need for his people to know about it. He would just keep it a secret between himself and David.

David leaned his head against his father's shoulder. He had a lot to say which was private and confidential, and fortunately Waffi could not understand English.

"Dad," he began, "has Mother told you about the baby yet?"

"Why, yes," answered Dad, smiling. "She told me about it a little while ago. Are you pleased, David?"

"Yes," said David. He was silent for a moment; then he said abruptly, "Dad, if Mother has a new baby she'll need me at home. Please, Dad, don't make me go away to boarding school. The baby will only be five months old, and I could go to day school here."

Dad said nothing for a time. They had reached the top of the hill and a great vista of hills and valleys stretched out in front of them. They could see the white road winding ahead for miles and miles.

"What are you going to be when you grow up, Davie?" said Dad at last.

"I'm going to be a missionary," answered David firmly, "and perhaps a doctor like you. But you could teach me that, couldn't you, Dad?"

Dad smiled and shook his head. "There are such things as exams," he said; "but in any case, you can't just choose to be a missionary. We are missionaries because God chose us. A missionary means that someone is sent to carry a message. God does not send everyone. If I want to do an operation I choose a knife that is clean and sharp and ready, and if you want to be chosen and used by God later on, then you must spend your time from now on getting ready."

"How?" asked David.

"Well," said Dad, "once, long ago, God wanted to

send an important message but He couldn't find a single grown-up who was ready to carry it, so He chose a boy—"

"Samuel," interrupted David eagerly.

"Yes, Samuel," said Dad, "because Samuel was ready. For years he had kept himself clean and pure and good, even though he lived with such wicked people. For years he had obeyed Eli, and swept the temple, and worked his very best even when everyone else was greedy and lazy. And because he was learning to serve God in that temple, he never cried to go home even though he only saw his mother once a year. And so God chose that clean, obedient, brave boy to be His messenger."

"There's a rabbit!" shouted Waffi without turning around.

"There was another time too," Dad went on, "when God wanted a king, but none of the tough, strong soldiers were ready, so God chose a shepherd boy."

"Me," said David with a chuckle.

"Yes, David," said Dad. "And why do you think God chose David?"

"Because he looked after his sheep so well," answered David as well as he could. They had turned onto the stony hill road and, being rather light, he was bouncing up and down in the most delightful manner.

"Yes," agreed Dad. "For years he'd been getting ready when no one was looking. There wasn't much he could do, but what there was he learned to do perfectly: to aim perfectly with his slingshot, and to play beautifully with his harp, and to fight great battles and kill lions and bears. No one was looking and no one would have known if he'd lost a lamb or two; but David was getting ready, and when

someone was needed suddenly to kill the giant, God chose
the boy who was used to winning battles in secret.''

"But couldn't I get ready here?'' said David, still bouncing.

"Not really,'' answered Dad. "There's no place here
where you could really do very well in your work. Getting
ready means being willing to be in the place where God
wants you, going on bravely and working your hardest—
being a shining light wherever you are. I hope you will
usually be with good people, but sometimes you may not
be. Then you'll have to be different, like Samuel.''

"Like 'a son of God without rebuke, in the midst of a
crooked, perverse nation,' '' said David.

"Yes,'' said Dad, rather surprised. "I'm glad you remembered that. When you get to school—''

"I saw a hedgehog,'' shouted Waffi, and at that, Dad had
to stop the car, and the two boys tumbled out to inspect it.
They wanted to wrap it in the car duster and take it back
to Joan, but in the end they let it go, partly because of its
fleas and partly because it might be a mother with a nest of
babies. So they started off again and watched for the red
rocks rising above the village. Soon they spied them, bright
in the morning sun, and as they neared the village a little
figure with a baby tied on her back stepped out from behind the olive trees and stood waving. It was Lela so they
stopped and left the car in the shade and she led them to
her master's house. She greeted them with shy love, but
she did not look happy. Her face was grave and troubled
and she walked ahead of them in silence.

Their host and hostess were waiting for them in the
cool mud house that smelled with the sweetness of dried
corn and herbs. The floor had been newly swept and bright

rugs had been laid for the guests. All was in order to welcome them, and delicious food was ready on the glowing charcoal outside, but even David sensed something wrong. The man was smiling and courteous, but the woman who served them looked anxious and tired. Once or twice she slipped out to the gate and spoke to someone in a whisper, and when the doctor addressed her she scarcely seemed to be listening. Without doubt, some shadow lay over the little home; yet not till their guests were properly rested and fed, did Lela's master speak of their troubles.

"My wife's sister is very sick," said the man. "She has been weak for a long time, but her husband made her carry the charcoal from the market last night. She fell under the load and now she lies on her mattress speaking to no one. If you are rested, could you go and see her? My wife will take you across. The sick of the village are coming after the village priest gives the prayer call."

"You should have told me sooner," said Dad, rising at once and noticing that the anxiety in the woman's face gave place to deep relief. "David and Waffi, come too. You can play outside."

They went out into the sunshine and down a hill where the marigolds were opening, to a little hut beside the river. The door was open and as they approached they could hear the sound of difficult, labored breathing, and the frightened crying of a child. The hut looked pitch-dark inside after they had been in the bright noonday. David and Waffi sat down on the step while the doctor went in.

He stayed there a long time. The children could hear him talking softly with Lela's mistress. Very soon Lela joined them with the two babies and sat down beside them. Some tiny kids came and nuzzled their hands and tried to push their way into the house, and some chickens pecked in the mud at their feet; but Lela sat with her chin resting in her hand, staring straight ahead of her.

"Why are you so sad, Lela?" asked Waffi. "Is the sick woman one of your family?"

Lela shook her head. "No," she answered, "she is one of my mistress' family."

"Then why do you weep?" insisted Waffi who knew nothing about sympathy.

"Because the woman who is sick has a daughter. If her mother dies, my mistress will take her, and what will become of me?" Lela broke into crying. "They will turn me out! Oh, if only I had died with my mother!"

She rocked herself to and fro hopelessly, and the little boys sat silent, not knowing what to say. But the older baby flung his arms around her neck and gave her some wet kisses, and the lean cat purred and rubbed against her legs. A baby goat with stubby horns nuzzled against her, and after a while she accepted their comfort and stopped rocking and crying. They sat silently in the kind spring sunshine till Dad reappeared, looking sad and grave.

"Is she going to die?" whispered David, slipping his hand into his father's.

"I'm afraid so," answered his father. "Probably very soon. There's nothing more I can do now. Her sister will stay and I will look in before we go home."

Lela could not understand, but she caught the tone of voice and her eyes darkened. For the second time in her life she would, no doubt, be left desolate. Although her master was not always kind, she had come to love her mistress and the two curly-haired brown babies. They did not make up for her own mother, but they were all she had.

Now someone else, she supposed, would take her in. Little servants were very useful.

They had reached her master's house where a crowd had gathered around the gate. The doctor went inside and sat down, and one by one they came to him. Some had terrible sores that needed cleaning and binding up. David and Waffi had gone off to the river, but Lela stayed near the doctor.

"It will take a long time to see all those people," she said suddenly. "See, I will dress the sores and put on the bandages for you."

"You?" said the doctor in surprise. "Do you know how?"

"Of course," said Lela. "I watched the nurses every day, and when I got better one of them used to let me help. See! First I wash my hands."

The doctor watched her in astonishment. She had spread a clean cloth on the little table, and was laying out the dressings with cleanly scrubbed hands. She did not look up again for she was intent on her task, cleaning a wound. He started to examine another patient, and when he turned back the limb was neatly bandaged.

"I was in the hospital twelve weeks," she reminded him. "Every day I watched and learned. Now I am almost a nurse."

"I believe you are," said the doctor thoughtfully. "Do you know how to put drops in eyes?"

"Oh, yes," answered Lela. "You wash your hands, so! And you tip the head back, so! You pull down the eyelid, so! Many, many times I watched."

"Good for you!" said the doctor, and he looked at her with new attention. For the first time that day she looked happy. In spite of her slightly twisted back she was quick and capable, and she knew what it was to be ill. They were terribly shorthanded at the hospital; he must talk it over with the nurses. Perhaps, if someone had time to train her, she might become very useful.

The last patient had been seen but the courtyard was still full, for a doctor did not come to the village often, and many who leaned against the house or squatted under the fig tree were just sightseers. Someone spread a sack, and the doctor sat down on it and drew out his New Testament. The people gathered closer, smiling and expectant. They felt no need for a new religion but it was interesting to hear about it. Lela crept up behind and sat with her sad little face cupped in her hands. Waffi and David, who had come back wet, warm, and dirty from the river, reclined on the ground with their arms around the dog's neck.

Dad spoke to them, and they all sat very still. Nothing moved except the creeping shadows as the sun sank toward the red rocks. He spoke about the God in whose presence is perfect joy, and a refuge from all fear. But they could never know Him or come to Him because there was something between—sin, which separates God and sinners forever.

Then he spoke about Jesus on the cross, who carried away our sins, who took them, like a great load, on Himself, and was punished for them, and died because of them.

"And," said Dad, holding up a handkerchief between himself and the man who squatted at his feet, "if this handkerchief is between me and you, and I take it away, what is now left between us?"

"Nothing," said the crowd, and they laughed delightedly, because that was an easy question, and they could all answer it.

"That's right," said Dad, "nothing! Just like the open way for any sinner who repents of his sins and believes that they have been taken away by Jesus. Jesus opened the way to God. We can run to our refuge."

A few turned away contemptuously. One laughed and another spat. But they mostly sat listening quietly while the doctor spoke of the refuge of the love of God. Lela listened, spellbound. He meant no more loneliness, no more desolation. She need never again say, "I have no one to love me."

And Waffi, with his head at the doctor's elbow, understood what he had to do. He would have to be done with stealing and lying and bad words, and trust in Jesus. And there would be no more horror, no fear of darkness and death. Jesus would be his Saviour and Comforter, in life and death, forever and ever.

The preaching came to a close, and everyone broke out talking or asking questions. Some had appeared while the talk was going on and were in a hurry for medicine. Two or three readers asked for books, and one young woman seemed thoughtful. But the doctor, looking around on their merry, careless faces, felt discouraged. Once again he had told the heartbreaking, glorious story of the Cross, and no one seemed moved by it.

But there were two little faces he did not see, because they were behind him and had withdrawn into the shadows. Lela's heart was glad with a new realization of love, and Waffi's beat fast with new courage and hope. The doctor did not know that through his message one troubled little boy had found his way to the Refuge, and one lonely girl had been comforted of all her desolation and fear.

CHAPTER 12

Out of the Shadows

LELA STOOD LOOKING after the car until it was only a little cloud of dust, far away where the road met the horizon. Then she turned and climbed the hill, limping a little because she was very tired. Never before, even on the day that her mother had died, had the future seemed quite so dark. She had only been a little child then, and she had known that someone would have to look after her somehow. But now she was older, and she had learned to be afraid. She knew now what life could be when she did not belong and was not wanted. It would be very well if she were strong and able to work, but sometimes the loads she had to carry were just too heavy for her, and her twisted back ached dreadfully. A new master might give her even heavier loads to bear, and a new mistress might be far less kind than the present one.

She sat on the root of an olive tree that straggled across the path, and looked back along the white road. It was dark now, but a sickle-shaped moon hung in the sky, and the silver leaves of the tree rustled softly. She had so longed for this day, and now it had come and gone. David, whom she loved, would be halfway home, his head snuggled against his father's shoulder, and she might never see him again. There were many little villages, and anyhow he was soon going to school.

She went over the events of the day, one by one, in her mind, lingering especially over that last hour—the group of men and women gathered around the doctor, listening attentively for the most part. He had talked about a Refuge, and Lela sat for a long time, her head resting on her knees, trying to remember every word. Jesus had taken away the barrier of sin. Jesus had opened the way to the Refuge. She could run, as it were, to those open arms of love. She need never feel lonely or forsaken again. She must not forget. Oh, if only she had the Book and could read about it!

She got up and hurried up the path. As she neared the hut she could hear her master calling angrily, and she realized with a start how long she had been.

"Lazy girl!" shouted her master, picking up his stick threateningly. "Running after strangers when you are needed at home. Go over to the house of my wife's sister and tell my wife to come. It is time she cooked my supper."

The older babies, unwashed and unfed, had fallen asleep, curled up together like two kittens on the mud floor. Lela, feeling very guilty, lifted them onto the mattress and covered them. Then she hurried down the hill to the hut by the river where a tiny oil lamp burned in the darkness.

The room was full of neighbors, but they sat very quietly, waiting for the change to come. Then they would wail and beat their breasts in hopeless grief. Lela hardly liked to break the silence by slipping in around the curtain to where her mistress crouched beside her sister. But no one seemed to notice her as she touched the woman gently on the shoulder. "Come," she whispered. "Your husband waits for you and orders you to come now."

The woman rose with a burst of tears, stooped to kiss the pale face, and followed Lela out into the night weeping. She longed to stay, but her husband must be obeyed. She would never see her sister again. Death would steal her away before she returned.

I wish they knew about heaven, thought Lela, hurrying along behind her mistress. *I wish they knew the verse I learned in the hospital: "Jesus said, I go to prepare a place for you." I wish they knew the hymn we learned at the ward service, "There is a beautiful country . . ." I wish someone would come back and tell them all. Then they would not weep and wail at death as they do now. I think I would not be sad to die. I think I would be glad to go to a beautiful home, because I shall never have a home here. Perhaps if I knew more I could tell them. But who would listen to a servant child?*

They had reached home by now. Lela's master sat half asleep, lulled by his pipe. No one spoke. His wife's silent sorrow shamed him a little, and he sat quietly while she prepared the meal. But neither she nor Lela were hungry, and the man ate alone.

Suddenly, the silence of the night was broken by the loud crying of a child, and a moment later the curtain was pulled aside and a girl of about twelve ran into the room and flung herself on the floor beside them.

"Dead!' cried the girl. "Gone! Oh, what shall I do? Where shall I go?"

Lela's mistress gave a cry too and gathered the child into her arms. They rocked to and fro, moaning and crying in their hopeless grief. Then the woman spoke through her tears without a single glance at her husband.

"You shall come to me, little one," she said. "Are you not my sister's child? Is not this your home?"

Her husband stopped cleaning the plate with his bread and looked up sharply.

"We cannot have two girls," he said. "If this one comes, Lela will have to go."

No one argued the point. Lela shrank into the shadows, and the moaning and crying went on softly. Then her mistress told her to clear the supper and, bidding good night to her husband, she went off to join the mourners in her sister's house.

Lela washed the bowl and lay down beside the sleeping babies, but she could not sleep. She knew that time was very short. Unless she could make up her mind, it would be made up for her very quickly. Once she got into the clutches of someone who needed her to work, she might never escape.

I will pray to God and ask Him to show me what to do, she said to herself. *If He truly loves me, He will show me. He will lead me to some refuge. I will pray, like they do in the hospital, with my eyes shut and my hands folded.* And so she lay, silently talking in her heart to the One she was beginning to know. And when she had told Him all about her trouble, and had asked Him to show her exactly what to do, she lay awake far into the night weighing in her mind all the possibilities. The priest of the village needed a servant and, unless God answered her prayer quickly, she would probably be given to him. He had two wives who quarreled all day long, and she felt she would rather die than go to him.

Yes, she would far rather die and go to the beautiful country whose gates were wide open to those whose sins had been forgiven. She had once asked David what it was like, but he had not been able to tell her much. He only knew that it was very, very beautiful, and he thought there was a river there, and the streets were made of gold. That, at least, would be smoother than the stony paths of the mountains.

Her thoughts wandered to that sunny winter afternoon when she had sat on the hospital sun porch in a wheelchair and David had sat on the wall swinging his legs. She could see him so clearly in her mind—his blue eyes and freckled face and rumpled fair hair. David—how she loved him! She lay thinking about him, smiling in the dark, and perhaps she fell asleep for she seemed to be standing at the bottom of a high hill, and it must have been early in the morning, because, although she was in a shadowed place, the crest of the hill was bathed in sunshine. She could see David far, far ahead, running upward toward the summit, very small and alone in those vast distances. And in her dream she called to him, and he turned back to see if she was following; and when he saw her, he pointed to the sunlight and beckoned her to come, and she began to climb the steep rough track. But she was moving fast, because she thought he was waiting for her.

"David," she cried, "wait for me! I'm coming." Then suddenly a great boulder seemed to leap from the mountain and strike her, and she woke, trembling and crying in the dark. But it was no boulder; it was just her master prodding her with his foot because she was crying out in her sleep.

She lay very still, although wide awake, and her master

lay down and was soon snoring. Her dream had faded, but her prayer had been answered and she knew perfectly and clearly now what she had to do. David had called her, and at the earliest opportunity she would go to him. She thought she could go that same morning because it was market day, and many traveled on the roads. She was so sure that this was her answer that she soon fell asleep and slept peacefully till daybreak. Then she crept from under the blanket she had shared with the babies, tied her few ragged garments into a bundle, and tiptoed out the door. Her mistress had come home and lay sleeping with the motherless girl in her arms.

Already the marketers were setting out, and Lela joined them. One or two asked her where she was going, and she told them that she had to go to the hospital. They supposed that the doctor had told her to come, so they showed no surprise.

"But it is a long way for a child like you with a twisted back," said their neighbor who was driving a horse loaded with sacks. "Come, you shall sit on the turnips until we reach the road."

Lela enjoyed her ride on the turnip sacks. The world looked rather like her dream: the valley path was still shadowed, but the sun was kissing the tops of the hills, and the dew lay thick on the grass. The horse was fresh, and trotted briskly along, passing bands of women bowed almost double under their loads of charcoal. The little mountain road was thronged with marketers, all trying to reach the town early; but the sunlight had crept down to meet them before they came in sight of the main road. By the time the town came into view, the sun had climbed high in the sky, and the houses were so white and the sea was so blue that Lela thought again of the bright city whose gates were closed to sin. Only she knew there was plenty of sin in the marketplace and was anxious to get away from it.

The kind neighbor put her down on the cobbles and pointed out the road to the hospital. Lela hesitated a moment, then she said, "Sir, will you speak a word to my master?"

"Yes, I will," said the neighbor. "I will say shame on him, to send a crippled child so far alone."

"No, no," said Lela, "he does not know I've come. But he has another girl now, and he does not want me. Tell him I am going to stay at the hospital. Tell him he need not ask for me because I have found a home. And may God have mercy on you."

The man was surprised. "Yes, I will give him your message." He started to unload his turnip sacks and Lela hurried through the streets that led to David. She had not really thought out what she was going to say. There was only one thing clear: David had called her, and she had come. But as she climbed the hill she began to feel uneasy. How would she explain? What if they had no room and told her to go back? They had sent her away from the hospital even when she wanted to stay very much indeed, because someone else needed her bed. Oh, what would she do if they sent her back now?

The thought slowed her eager feet. When she reached the hospital gate she stopped. People were going in and out, and nobody was asked to stay. Perhaps she would wait a little until she felt calmer. She wandered along the road, then went along the side of the road to the cliff top. She sat down in the very place where she had lain so ill before David had led her master to the hospital. Staring out over the sea, her head resting on her arms, she gave herself up to her hopes and fears.

She forgot that she had had nothing to eat all day except a raw turnip which she had nibbled on the journey, for she was hungry and thirsty for something more than food. If only she knew more about God, her Refuge; if only she knew what He wanted her to do; if only she could read the Book where all the secrets of His love and comfort were written down so plainly. But would anyone ever have time to teach her to read? She was too old to go to school, and the nurses were all so busy, and David was too young. If she could read, then she would not mind going back so much. She felt she could face anything if she could only read from that Book.

Worn out by her sleepless night, her longing, and her hunger, she fell fast asleep, and slept long and deeply. When she awakened, the sun was going down over the sea. She jumped up quickly, for she no longer had any choice of what to do. It was too late to go back to the village, and she could not stay out at night. She must go to the doctor's house now, whether she liked it or not.

She wandered slowly toward the hospital, and by the time she reached the gate it was getting dark and passersby looked at her curiously, wondering why she stayed so late in the road. She turned and walked through the gate, but when she reached the house she did not knock at the door. She stepped aside and peeped in at the window where the light was shining.

David's mother sat on the couch, with Joan on her lap and David and Waffi at her feet. She was reading to them from the Book, and blue eyes and black eyes were fastened on her. In her longing to hear, Lela forgot her shyness. She walked straight in at the door without knocking at all, and sat down beside the little boys.

They were greatly surprised to see her and wanted to ask all sorts of questions but she silenced them with a wave of her hand. "Go on," she said, "and let me listen. Afterward I will tell you all."

So they went on, and she heard for the first time the story of the sisters at Bethany weeping for their dead brother and how Jesus turned their sorrow to joy. Lela's thoughts flew back to the wailing women in the village, and the poor sufferer who died in the dark and had never heard the name of Jesus or known about eternal life. Oh, if only they knew! Had no one the time to go and tell them? She turned sharply on David as the story drew to a

close. "Are there many people in your country?" she asked.

"Hundreds!" said David. "In fact, I think millions. Why?"

"Can they all read that Book?" demanded Lela.

"Yes, everyone can read in England," answered David proudly.

"Then why don't they come and tell us all?" cried Lela. "What are they doing? No one in our village knows anything about it."

"I suppose they are too busy doing other things," said David. "Or perhaps they don't know."

"Well, teach me to read," said Lela decidedly, "and I will go back and tell them when I'm older."

"But they won't listen to you," put in Waffi softly. "If my father knows I'm a Christian he'll punish me. I haven't told him yet, and if I do he'll be very angry. I don't think he'll let me learn anymore."

"But when they see that you are willing to be punished for it, and that Jesus is so precious to you that you won't give up even if you are punished, then they will begin to believe," said David's mother. And then she forgot all the questions she was going to ask Lela; she even forgot David and Joan. She forgot everything except the two little disciples sitting at her feet, drawn by the love of Christ into a path which, if followed, must lead at times to bitter loneliness and persecution. And leaning forward, she began to teach them, as clearly as she possibly could, how great things they must suffer for His name's sake.

CHAPTER 13

When the Sun Rose

A RE YOU AWAKE, David?" said Dad softly, because he was too excited to wait any longer. "I've got something to show you."

David turned sleepy, blue eyes from the window where the dawn was flaming over the sea. He was only just waking from a complicated dream, but the moment he saw Dad's face he knew what had happened, and he tumbled out of bed into his father's arms.

"Peter or Rose?" asked David.

"Peter," said Dad, "so you've got your wish." David tried not to feel too pleased, because the others had really hoped for Rose. But Peter would grow up and come to school and play football and be a friend. David had forgotten that by that time he himself would be nearly grown up. He was running out in his bare feet, with his pajamas falling off him, when his father stopped him.

"Gently, David," he said. "Mother's very tired and it's very early. Just go in and kiss her, and take a look at Peter, and then let's all go to sleep again. Mother and I have had a bad night."

So David went in on tiptoe and found Mother leaning back on her pillows having a cup of tea. A nurse was there also having a cup of tea, and they'd poured out one for

Dad. Peter lay like a small sausage roll, his black, downy head peeping out from one end of his shawl. Peter or Rose —there didn't seem to be much difference either way at this stage. David stared at him for a long time and then stooped and kissed the soft little head. Then he snuggled up to his mother on the bed and thought how happy they all were. He suddenly felt terribly sorry for Murray, stuck far away in England, shut out from this warm circle of family love. He even wished the kind nurse would go away and leave him alone with Mother and Dad and Peter. He would have liked Joan too, but she was too little to understand how important it was to be very quiet and sensible, and was probably better asleep.

They gave him a cup of tea and a cookie, just like a grown-up, and the daylight came stealing in through the back windows. Some birds twittered, and the smell of the Easter lilies that grew up against the windows drifted in on them. It was only four days to Easter, a good time for a baby to be born!

He thought he would like to stay there forever with Mother's arm around him, and Peter snuffling and making little sounds in the cradle. But Dad picked him up and carried him back to bed, and five minutes later he was fast asleep in the early morning sunshine. They all slept and slept, and by the time they woke David was late for school. He took a note to the school teacher to explain. He was rather scared, but when she heard what had happened she understood and gave him a holiday. It was the last day before Easter vacation anyway.

There was a lot to do with Mother in bed. The children ran all around the hospital to make sure that everyone knew about Peter. The first person they met was Lela.

Lela wore a uniform now and helped in the wards and everyone was glad she had come. She lived with Rabia the cook, who was a Christian and was teaching her to read.

Lela had heard the news and was radiant and longing to come and peep. Her face seemed to get happier every day, and the patients loved her, for she had known what it was to be sick, and she was very gentle with them.

David helped all day long. He played with Joan and went to the store and dried the dishes, and every time Mother woke up he ran in to tell her that all was well and that she could stay in bed with the baby as long as she liked. He adored the baby. Peter was so tiny and red and crumpled, and that evening he and Joan were allowed to sit on the bed and hold him in turns. Peter blinked at David wisely and yawned. Then Lela arrived with a bunch of roses, and she too was allowed to hold Peter.

Her work for the day was finished, so they sat down on the step together, and once again Waffi joined them because Mother always read with the two boys in the evenings. But Mother was too tired that night, so they just sat together, the three of them, while Dad put Joan to bed.

"Ah, David," said Lela, smiling, "you won't want to go to your country now. You have a little brother to look after."

David frowned. The same thought had been tugging at his heartstrings all day. "Next year when I am there I think Mother and Dad are coming to England," he said stoutly. "They are going to stay a long time. Perhaps we will all stay there together and not come back till I am big."

He knew this was not true, for Mother and Dad only intended to stay for nine months. But after all, a lot of

things might happen by that time and they might be persuaded to change their minds.

But Waffi was frowning, and Lela's eyes were big with horror. There was a moment's silence.

"Who will go on teaching me about being a Christian if your mother goes?" asked Waffi flatly.

"And who will go to the sick people in the villages, and who will teach them about God, if your father goes?" said Lela.

"The others," said David uncomfortably, but he knew that wasn't really true either. There weren't nearly enough of them. No one had time to do anyone else's work, only their own. Perhaps Rabia would help Waffi; but there were dozens and dozens of little villages where no one had ever been to preach the gospel—miles and miles of darkness where no light had ever shone.

Dad called David, and he said good night and went indoors. The nurse was looking after Mother and he was
only allowed to go in for a minute or two in his pajamas to
say good night. He was feeling rather gloomy, but Dad
cheered him up by reminding him that it was Easter Sunday in three days' time. He asked if David would like to
go with him to the sunrise service up the mountain.

There was a sunrise service every year, but David had
never been before because he had been too small. But
now that he was nine, he was quite ready to attend such
affairs, and on Saturday night he went to bed early with
his Sunday clothes all laid out, ready for the morning.
Joan and Ragbag had not been told, as they would have
wanted to go too.

Dad woke him at 5:30 and he scrubbed himself in cold
water till he shone, and dressed in his clean white shirt
and navy corduroys. It was getting light over the sea but
the sun had not yet risen. They had a quick glass of milk
and a piece of bread and jam together and then crept out
of the house, leaving Mother, Joan, Peter, and Ragbag fast
asleep. Several people wanted a ride up the mountain, so
they set off with a full load, driving as fast as they dared
up the narrow twisting road, because they had to race the
rising sun, and the day was getting brighter every moment.

They got there just in time. The last steep turn brought
them around the corner of the mountain, and there below
them stretched the ocean through the fringe of eucalyptus
trees. Two big liners were just sailing away into the morning mists. They might round the cape or they might con-
tinue their far unbroken journey westward. But as soon
as the car stopped, everyone jumped out and faced east to
where the sun would rise over the island. There were

about fifty people of different nationalities collected on the green plateau with a steep slope of Easter lilies just below them. They were all watching the bright spears of morning shooting up above the rock, and suddenly the tip of the sun appeared and everybody burst out singing "Christ the Lord Is Risen Today."

David knew that hymn and sang with all his might,

> Now He bids us tell abroad
> How the lost may be restored,
> How the penitent forgiven,
> How we too may enter heaven.
> Alleluia!

Lela would like this hymn, thought David. She had once said, "Why didn't you come sooner and tell us about the way to heaven?" David didn't know the answer to that, and he looked across to the headland where the north coast continues around the turn and becomes the west coast. It was studded with little villages, and none of their people had ever been told.

But the hymn was finished, and someone was reading the Bible—the Easter story in the sixteenth chapter of Mark. Early on Sunday morning when the sun was rising over the Sea of Galilee, and the dew lay on the shadowed flowers, just as it did now, they had seen the open tomb and the young men in shining clothing and had heard the greatest news ever proclaimed: "He is risen!"

David remembered how he had told that story to Lela, and her sad little face had lit up with amazed joy. No one had ever told her before that Jesus was alive. It had made all the difference in her lonely life.

His straying thoughts came back to the reading. The

chapter was nearly finished, and the last command of the Lord Jesus rang out clear and strong:

"Go ye into all the world, and preach the gospel to every creature."

"Go and tell everyone." The sun had swung clear of the island now, and the sunlight had crept down the crag, bathing the little villages in warmth and brightness. *That is what happens when you preach the gospel,* thought David. *People who are sad and sinful will suddenly see the way and feel the comfort of Jesus' love. That's what we're here for—to shine like lights in the world—for these towns and little villages where the name of Jesus as Saviour had never been heard.*

"And the disciples went forth and preached everywhere" —out into all the places where no one had ever been to tell before. David felt a little tingle of excitement. Of course they mustn't go home! Mother and Dad would stay and tell people. Lela and Waffi would grow up and learn and go and tell. He and Murray would be in England, getting ready; they would grow up too, to be brave, faithful disciples, "sons of God without rebuke." Then they would come back and spread the light farther and farther. Even Joan and the little new baby would be old enough some day—His imagination was running riot now, and when he looked around the whole hillside was drenched in sunshine. He could not see a shadow anywhere.